THE
ENCHANTERS'
CHILD

• NAVYA SARIKONDA •

First Paperback/eBook Edition: December 2018

ISBN 978-0-9980256-0-5 (Softcover/Paperback)

ISBN 978-0-9980256-1-2 (Hardcover/Paperback)

ISBN 978-0-9980256-2-9 (eBook)

Library of Congress Control Number: 2018913191

ACKNOWLEDGEMENTS

Writing this book was a long process and wouldn't have been possible without the amazing people that have helped and encouraged me along the way.

Firstly, I want to thank my family. Ever since I started writing, they've been there as a supporting force and encouraged me to keep writing in those moments when I doubted myself. They have stood with me through the ups and the downs. I want to specifically thank my father, who without, this book wouldn't have been possible. He spent late nights and long hours searching for editors, publishers, and others to make my book possible and for that I will forever be grateful.

A special thanks to Ann Howard Creel, my editor, who helped me grow in my writing and provided valuable mentorship during the editing stages of my book. I want to also give thanks to Cheyenne DeBorde for helping me improve my book further by offering another perspective and advice.

And to everyone else who has given encouragement and shown enthusiasm for this book. It means more than you can know.

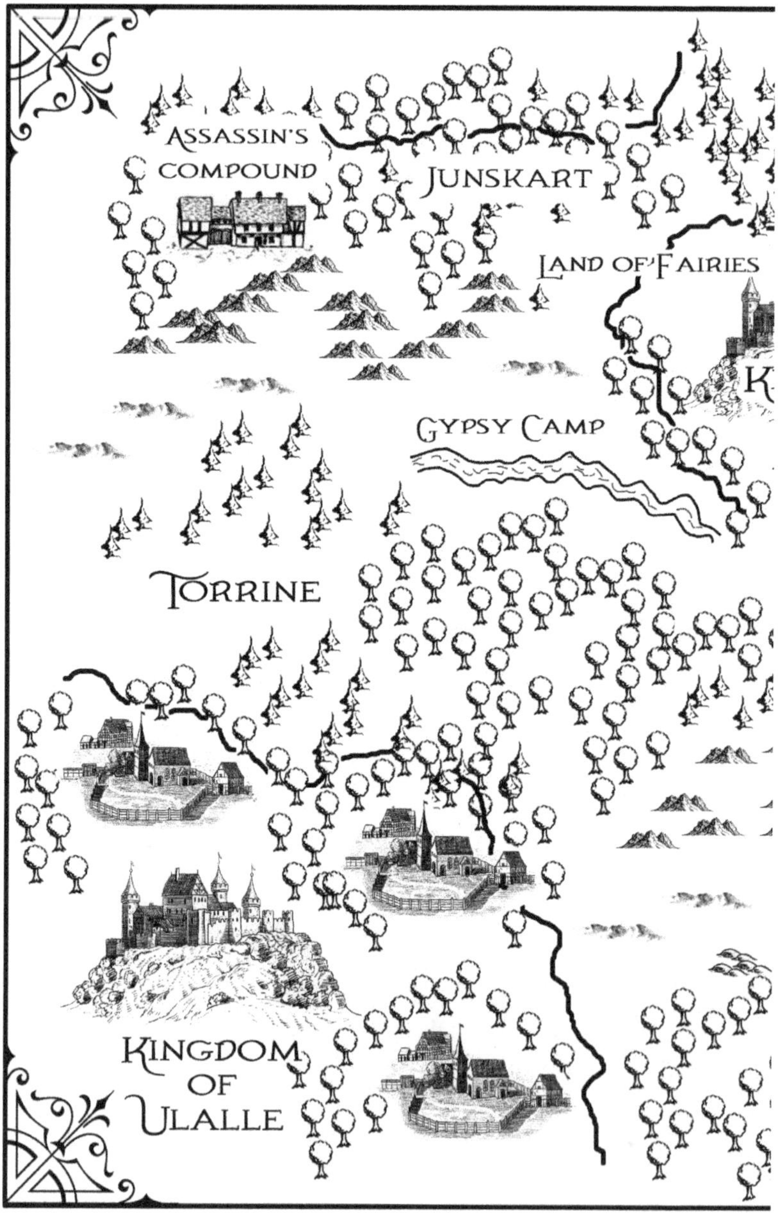
ASSASSIN'S COMPOUND
JUNSKART
LAND OF FAIRIES
GYPSY CAMP
TORRINE
KINGDOM OF ULALLE

CHAPTER 1
WREN

I LOOK AROUND THE dark room, my muscles clenched in fear as a dead silence ascends. Frantically, I run my hands against the cold wall behind my back in search for a door, but to no avail. Wondering where I am, I hold my breath and take a small step into the center of the room. Just as I am about to shout for help, I hear the soft sound of a human voice. I freeze, motionless.

I think I imagined it, when the voice starts again. As it gets louder, I realize with a chill what it's saying.

"*Come and find me. Come and find me.*"

As I swivel my head around the room, trying to find the source, my eyes catch on a movement. As my vision adapts to the darkness, I realize that it's the shadow of a person.

I jolt awake, and my eyes open to see the brown ceiling of the cottage. Sitting up, I try to ignore the layer of sweat beginning to make my chemise stick to my skin.

The nightmare visits me in my sleep more often than ever these days, no matter how hard I try to forget about it.

I get up from the bed and wince as my feet hit the cold, dirt floor. I look around the room; most people would think it's not much, but I feel lucky to call it my own. The only object in the room, other than the bed, is a worn-out chest holding my clothes. As I make my way into the main room of the cottage, the smell of familiar herbs hits me. The room is empty, and I know that Aunt Adnis has already gone. I pick up my satchel, as well as the basket filled with herbs, before putting on my tattered cloak and leaving the cottage.

Dew sprinkles the grass and a mist settles in the air as I walk down the silent pathway. Crickets still chirp into cold morning air and I take a deep breath in an attempt to forget about my nightmare. I pass a few more cottages before I reach the center of the village. It isn't much, but the tiny square is enclosed by shops holding the necessities that we thrive on. Despite the early hour, the square is already filled with people, buying what they need and trying to sell their wares. I endeavor to ignore the grumbling of my stomach as I walk past the bakery and head toward the stall at the other side of the square, where Aunt Adnis is selling our herbs.

After my parents died, she is the only family I have. Aunt Adnis is the closest thing I have to my father, with her chestnut-brown hair and emerald-green eyes.

When I approach, she gives me a gentle smile. "Here," she says as she hands me a few coins. "We need some more bread."

While she palms the money to me, I feel the weight of being watched. Brushing off the feeling, I walk toward the bakery. On my way, I feel something pulling my satchel. Alarmed, I turn around to see a man reaching inside of it. My mind immediately goes to the photo of my parents that rests within. In a moment of panic, I do something that I immediately regret. Feeling magic on my fingertips, I touch his shoulder and a blue hue emits into the air before it slams the man into the wall behind him. He lets out a loud grunt before sliding onto the ground, unconscious. I immediately feel the blood rush out of my face as I look around, hoping that no one has noticed. But, to my horror, a few passersby pause, staring at the man in confusion.

A short lady with a kind face steps up to me. "What happened to him?"

Relief floods through me. "I- I don't know," I blurt out quickly as I push through them to head back toward Aunt Adnis. While they may not have seen it, someone else might have. Once the man gains consciousness, he surely will remember.

Crossing the square in a blur, I reach the stall where Aunt Adnis is handing over a vial of herbs to a customer. When she sees me rushing toward her, her eyebrows dip in concern. I wait until the customer leaves before explaining what happened. A flash of fear crosses her face before she grabs me by the sleeve, dragging me out of the square.

I protest, shocked. "What about the herbs?"

"Forget about the herbs. They're not important."

Before I know it, we're back at the cottage. Aunt Adnis

throws the door open, nudging me inside. "If anyone saw what happened, you're in danger. You have to leave."

I step back in shock. "What?"

She rushes around the cottage, quickly placing some food and water into a satchel. As she rushes by me, I grab her shoulders. "Don't you think this is a bit sudden?"

She looks at me, and I feel her muscles relax. "We can't take a risk. Go to the town, and find the Gavreel Society. You know what to do from there."

I look at my hands in disgust. I don't want this, I never wanted this. My magic rips away at my chance to be normal. I gulp down my panic, and put my hands on her shoulder as I tell her, "Come with me."

She shakes her head. "I need to stay here. This is your journey, and I will slow you down."

She opens her palm to reveal my mother's necklace. It is made up of a simple string, but the true beauty and power lies in the blue stone hanging from it. She ties it around my neck. When I look into her eyes, I see they're filled with pride and hope.

"Find the Sorcerer. Find the person who killed your parents," she says, vehemently.

She's about to lead me to the door when we hear the sound of a stampede of horses growing closer. I watch as Aunt Adnis' face turns as pale as a ghost, and I feel her tremble beneath my hands as she stares at the door in horror.

"Aunt Adnis? What's wrong?" I ask, panicked.

My voice quickly snaps her out of her trance, and

without removing her gaze from the door, she pushes me toward our small closet.

"Hide," she says tersely.

"What?" I shake my head, confused.

"Hide!" she repeats, and this time when she looks at me, I see pure fear in her eyes.

I force my legs to move toward the closet. As soon as I slip inside, I hear a loud bang behind me. A lump forms in my throat as I peek through the tiny slit I have left between the closet door and the wall.

The front door of our cottage lies on the floor, broken. In the doorway stand a handful of figures. I squint to try and make out any of their faces when I realize that they don't have any. In fact, as I continue to stare, I realize that the outline of their bodies seems to blend into the wall behind them. Shadows. Immediately my mind turns to a flashback of Aunt Adnis' warning before she started to secretly teach me how to control my magic and use it if required.

Don't use your magic in front of anyone, or the Shadows of Dark will follow close behind.

I had always thought that the Shadows of Dark she referred to represented danger in a figurative way, but as I stare at the black figures, I slowly realize that she meant it in a literal sense. The figure at the front of the group steps forward and looks at something outside of my view. Aunt Adnis.

"Where is she?" the figure asks. His voice is a hollow thing, void of emotion.

I hold my breath as I wait for Aunt Adnis to answer. "She is gone." Her calm voice rings out.

The figure steps even closer to where I imagine Aunt Adnis is. "Do you know the punishment for providing housing to a magic wielder?"

His question is met with a brief silence before Aunt Adnis answers with a whisper. "She is just a child."

The shadow shakes his head. "Magic is prohibited."

Before I have time to react, he quickly pulls out his sword, and I hear a scream. I look on, wide-eyed in horror, as he pulls back a sword covered in blood.

"Search the room," he says.

A new wave of panic washes over me, and I look around frantically for a way to escape before realizing that I am trapped. The only way out is the front door. The shadows start to make their way across the house, turning things over as they go, and I watch as one of them head in the direction of the closet.

A sudden idea comes to my mind as the shadow inches toward me. I hurry to conjure up the spell that Aunt Adnis taught me a few months ago. It was one of the harder spells, and it still doesn't work for me at times. I try to push down the panic as I conjure up the invisibility spell. Being a spell that requires a lot of energy, it will only last for a couple of minutes at most.

Hopefully, a couple of minutes are all I need.

I reach inside of me, finding that familiar sliver of magic that has caused so much pain in my life, and call to it. It immediately reacts to my request, and I whisper the words required for the spell. The power of the spell causes the magic to almost slip, but I squeeze my eyes, and hold on to it. I feel a sudden burst in my chest, and I hesitantly open my eyes to see a shiny transparent sheet in front of me. The magic has worked. At that very moment, the door of the closet is swung open, and I find myself staring back into the eyes of one of the shadows.

For a second, I feel a jab of fear, thinking he can see me. But then his eyes roam to the rest of the closet before closing it. I let out a small breath of relief as I hear someone say, "She was telling the truth. The girl is gone."

I hear the door of the cottage close as they leave.

I wait with bated breath, for what seems like hours, until I am sure that they are truly gone before slipping out of the closet. Eyes burning, I force myself to look at where I remember Aunt Adnis was standing when I last saw her. I look in shock, as there is only a black circle on the floor where she once stood. The work of magic. A fresh wave of tears runs down my face as I crumble in front of the circle, the numbing shock wearing off.

CHAPTER 2
ZAYNE

WE ALL STAND around the table, looking at each other with sober eyes. We had just received news from one of our scouts that six new bodies were found in Torrine, dead.

I take a deep breath, keeping the worry at bay. "So, what's the plan?"

Asher, my closest friend, looks at me. "We could go to Torrine and see if we can find anything."

I shake my head. "Any traces would be gone by now; any tracks would have been washed away by the rain."

Noel speaks up. "We could set a trap, lure them to us."

Isa interrupts, "That's putting innocent lives in danger. We can't stoop that low."

I nod. "Isa is right. That's a last resort, and we are not even sure it will work."

Asher softly suggests, "We could try to find the Enchanters' Child."

I frown. Not again. "We've been over this. It's a children's story."

Asher frowns back. "We don't know that. Think about it. If we find the Enchanters' Child, he or she can help and maybe stop these deaths. There have been rumors going around that they really do exist."

I run my hand through my hair in frustration. "Any other ideas?" I met with silence. "We'll meet up in two days. If we find nothing, we have no choice but to go with Noel's plan."

Isa flinches but doesn't say anything, and I see Asher's jaw clench. I press my lips into a thin line and, without a word, I turn and exit the room. As I push out the door, I enter the stuffy back room connected to Noel's library.

The cool air hits me as I make my way back to the inn. It's my first time in Ulalle in a year and I had hoped that being back with the team would have helped me make progress, but it hasn't been the case. More deaths are occurring more frequently and I can tell that the group is losing hope. Hopefully a solution would present itself, and quickly.

I enter the inn, and immediately I'm blanketed by laughter and noise the opposite of what I feel inside. I quickly pick a table in the corner and watch the people around me. At one table, several men are huddled around, doing what seems to be gambling. Their easy smiles and loud laughter fills the inn, and I smile bitterly, remembering how, once, it was that easy for me to be happy. I order a drink and, as I wait, I notice a cloaked figure enter the inn. I tilt my head as the figure barely glances at the room before quickly making its way into the kitchen. I rub my face, exhausted. These days, there's little that I trust.

CHAPTER 3
QUINN

S WEAT RUNS DOWN my neck as I sprint another lap. The training room is going to close in a few minutes. I push myself harder and harder as I try to use the pain as a distraction from my memories. No such luck. I can still remember the flashing teeth of the creature as it killed my parents, and it has haunted me ever since. Shaking my head, I return back to the present. As I finish my lap, I hear footsteps echo against the stone floor. I turn around to see Walker.

"Damien summoned you, Quinn," he says.

I nod at him and he leaves. I look down at my sweat-covered clothes and frown. Nothing I can do about it now. When Damien summons you, he expects no delay. I walk out of the room and into the stone corridor. Other than the torches lighting the corridor, there are no decorations. Damien started the Compound years ago in secret. He trains the best assassins here. Myself being the best of the best, of course. I'm not being arrogant, I'm just telling the truth.

Finally, I arrive at the Hall doors, which are made of wood, and a picture of the Forbidden War is engraved on the surface. Any other person would be downright terrified if they had been summoned, but Damien summons me all the time to find information, or people, for him. I'm itching to get out of here; it's been forever since Damien has had a mission for me, and I hope that is why he called. I pull my shoulders back, lift my chin high, and knock on the door.

"Come in," a muffled voice says. I quietly open the door and slip into the Hall.

The Hall is a place for big meetings; it has a wooden table running along its length. During the times we have no meetings, this is the place where Damien summons people. I look around the room to find the man himself sitting at the end. Damien, reclining on the chair with his feet on the table, looks at me with his ice-blue eyes that seem to always be set into a steel glare.

"You summoned me?" I ask, while I bow, as is custom.

Damien dismisses my words with a wave of his hand. "Away with the formalities, Quinn. You never cared for them, so why start now?"

I answer him with a wolfish grin and rise from my position. "So, what will it be now?"

Damien looks at me and gravely says, "What I'm about to tell you now shall never be told to anyone else, understand? If I hear you have betrayed my wishes, I will kill you myself."

Always the polite gentleman.

I nod, and he continues, "I'm sure you're very well aware of the darkness slowly reaching the kingdom?"

Of course I am; a Sorcerer is said to be the cause of it, but I have no idea what that has to do with me. In good sense, however, I say none of this aloud.

Continuing, Damien says, "I want control over it."

His words send a course of shock through me. Obviously he would; it's always about more power when it comes to Damien, but this? It's impossible. I press my lips tightly together and say nothing. Comments would result in a flogging or, I cringe inside, worse.

"To accomplish this, of course, I need someone with powerful magic in their blood to do it for me. Naturally, magic was banished years ago and most have forgotten about it. Unfortunately, I need that someone to have been trained. The only person that's like this, except the Sorcerer, is the Enchanters' Child. There's a rumor that she or he is alive and trained, and I'm willing to take the risk. Regrettably, I'm not the only one looking for this person. There are many who are – one of them being the Sorcerer. As of now, he doesn't have enough power to do a lot of damage, but with the Enchanters' Child, he will gain more power than one can possibly imagine. I need you to find this person before anyone else does. Find the Enchanters' Child, and then I will give you your freedom. Perhaps also… I will even give you your sister."

His words echo through the Hall as the full weight of that statement sinks in. My freedom and my sister. Damien knew I would do anything for her. Even more-so, no one in the Compound has ever been offered his or her freedom; this Enchanters' Child must be important and near impossible to find.

My freedom. That is something I forgot even existed. It is a dream long diminished. But now that it is once again within my grasp, I will do anything to get it. I have no heart. I have no soul. I am not weak. I am the Black Assassin.

CHAPTER 4
WREN

I STARE AT THE necklace in my hand with a now familiar numbness. Aunt Adnis and I had planned to come together to town the following day for Trading Day, and to possibly find the Gavreel Society, but now I'm on my own.

I let out a shaky breath and force myself to leave my room in the inn. Alba hadn't noticed that anything was wrong when I arrived at the Blue Castle Inn yesterday. As head chef of the inn, she was quite busy when I walked in. When I quickly told her Aunt Adnis wasn't with me after she inquired about her whereabouts, she hadn't questioned a thing.

Over the years, Aunt Adnis and I had stayed at the inn during the annual Trading Day, and because we didn't have enough money, we would exchange lodging for work in Alba's kitchen. Because it's too early for the kitchen to be open, I have time to walk around town and see what I can find.

Wrapping my cloak tighter, I step out into the streets. My knowledge of the Gavreel Society includes that they have spies constantly looking out and reporting back to the group, specifically their leader, Francis. Somehow, I have to get their attention. I clench the letter inside my pocket and pray that my strategy will work. Because it's early, not many people are in town, despite it being Trading Day. This way it will be easier for me to be noticed, but I have to take care not to be noticed by the wrong people. Because this is the town in which the Society stays, there are bound to be more scouts here, watching.

I arrive at the deserted square as fog starts to settle in the air. Folding into myself, I make my way near one of the walls. I wait there for what seems like hours but can't be more than a couple of minutes when I feel someone watching me. I glance at the roof to see a figure crouching. I pull my hood down, cautious, before pulling the letter out of my pocket. Somehow, I know that they're who I'm seeking. My hand shakes as I slowly lift the letter into the light before dropping it to the ground. Without a word, I quickly leave the square.

After my morning shift at the inn, I make my way back to the square. The deserted area has been replaced with hundreds of carts and stalls for people selling their wares. I notice a blacksmith's forge wagon and, intrigued, I go up to it. My gaze is immediately drawn to the daggers and I pick one up for inspection. It is better than a lot of weapons I have at home and, as I look around, I see that all the other weapons are forged with mastery. The dagger I am holding is crafted painstakingly and the edges are sharp.

I hear a chuckle behind me, followed by a deep voice that asks, "Know how to use that?"

I whip around and see a man around my age, looking at me with blue eyes filled with amusement. He is wearing a crimson-red cloak, but otherwise, he's all in black. The only color standing out is his golden hair. His clothes are of rich material, so he must be wealthy.

I raise my eyebrows and reply, "You really shouldn't underestimate me."

He laughs again as if he finds me amusing. My stomach clenches at the sound and I feel an odd sensation in response. *If only he knew what I am capable of,* I think in amusement.

"Fancy daggers?" he asks. I nod, and he says, "I, personally, prefer the bow and arrow."

Like I asked. I roll my eyes and I turn back, hoping he will go away. No such luck. He approaches to the cart and picks up a smoothly carved bow. I watch him carefully as he examines it, and I see that he is no amateur.

"I'm impressed. Most wealthy people don't want anything to do with weapons. As I recall, they think of it as below them," I tell him.

He smiles as if he knows a joke I don't, and says, "Well, I'm not like most."

I let the comment slide and look at the blacksmith. "I'll be buying this."

The blacksmith, a big man with a kind face, smiles

and tells me the price. I wince at the amount and realize I can't buy it.

"Here, I'll pay for it. I'm buying the bow anyway." The cloaked man hands over the money, and I look at him, startled. No nobleman would gift an item to a peasant without expecting something in return.

I shake my head. "I can't pay you back."

He waves it off and replies, "No need."

As he turns to leave, I can't stop myself. "Why? Why would you do something like this? Nobody as rich as you would do something like this for me."

He turns back around and says, "I have done some bad things in my life and I like to think there is still good left in me." Then he turns and melts into the crowd.

I stare after him in confusion. What could he have possibly done? Shaking my head, I hurry to the inn.

CHAPTER 5
ZAYNE

As I WALK around town, I think of the deaths in Torrine. It is getting worse. Whatever the reason for these deaths, the killer is becoming more dangerous. More people were killed this week than in all of last month. Frustration rushes at me; how many more deaths until it stops, if it ever will stop? We have to find a way to end this, soon.

I'm so caught up in my thoughts that I suddenly bump into someone. I look up from the ground to apologize and see a girl around my age looking up at me. She has brown hair, a shade or so lighter than mine, and grey, stormy eyes filled a deep sadness. My breath catches as I wonder what must have caused that emotion, and it's then when I realize those eyes are familiar to me. I don't know how, but I do. She blinks and, just like that, it's gone.

"Alas, I didn't see you there." I apologize. She remains silent, her mouth set into a pout. She kneels to pick something up, and, when I look down, I see that she has dropped books I hadn't noticed before. I flinch and kneel down as well to help her. After she gathers all the books back into her arms, she stands up, not bothering to wipe the dirt off her peasant gown. She has probably come from a village for Trading Day.

Once again, I apologize, "I'm sorry."

She hesitates and then smiles.

"It's fine." Her voice comes strong and steady.

I don't know why, maybe it was that feeling like I knew her; I stretch my hand out and say, "I'm Zayne."

Slowly, she reaches to accept the shake. Her hand is enveloped in mine and is hard to the touch, with many nicks in it.

I wait for her to tell me her name, but the reply never comes. An awkward silence envelops us and I shuffle on my feet.

"Well, I'll see you around then." For an unknown reason, disappointment seeps into me.

I turn to leave, but then I hear her voice; it's so quiet that I almost miss it. "I'm Wren."

I look over my shoulder to answer, but she is gone. I shake my head and start to walk away. Deciding that I had nothing else to do with my time for now, I walk to the bookstore. Maybe, I can find something helpful there.

In no time, I enter the bookstore and immediately see John at his usual place behind the counter in the back, reading a newspaper. He doesn't look up as he tells me, "Someone left a letter for you. I have no idea how he or she knew where to send it, but I'm going to guess you told them."

I frown and ask him, "Who was it?"

"No name. I didn't read it; all I know is that it is addressed to you."

I walk up to the counter and he hands the letter to me without a word. Confused, I walk up the rusty, wooden stairs to the floor above as I stare at the letter in my hands. I unfold it. It's a small paper, one that had just enough space for what the writer wanted to say.

The "letter" was brief, saying: "Francis, please meet me at the gazebo in the Favian Gardens as soon as possible."

Francis is the name used for me when someone knows about the Gavreel Society but doesn't know my real identity. That means that whoever wrote this knows about the Gavreel Society. Fear shoots through me, but I push it down. It's probably just another member of the Society from my kingdom.

Curious, I know that I'm willing to go, but I am not going alone and, besides, the note never said anything about not bringing anyone.

"Are you sure this is a good idea?" Asher asks, later, as we approach Favian Gardens.

"No," I admit. "But I have to know what this person wants to tell us. It might be helpful.

"Or it might kill us," Asher mumbles, and I roll my eyes even though, inside, I agree with him.

"Do you even know who this person is?" Asher asks.

"No."

Asher sighs. "This could be a trap."

"Yes, I know."

"And there is no way I can talk you out of this?"

"Correct."

"That's what I thought."

Finally, we both reached the gardens and I realize that nobody is there presently. Seeing that the timing is set on purpose, along with the location, this person is smart. Asher and I walk down one of the fresh dirt paths, which all seem to lead to the center of the garden. The warm, early autumn air kisses my skin, and all around us is an array of gold and red which reminds me of fire. As the gazebo comes into view, our steps become slower and more cautious. The gazebo itself is small and has stone benches hugging the walls. As we climb the mossy stone steps, I see a figure with its back to us. They are wearing all black and I can barely distinguish their outlines. I hold my breath as they turn at the sound of our footsteps. The person I see is someone I wouldn't have expected in my wildest dreams.

"Wait, Wren? What are you doing here? It's not safe!" I tell her as I look around in worry. The person who sent me the letter can arrive at any moment.

"I'm waiting for someone. What are you doing here?" she asks disbelievingly, looking confused as she glances from me to Asher.

"I'm meeting someone."

Realization dawns upon us at the same time. "You don't happen to be 'Francis,' do you?" she asks with incredulity.

"You're the one who wrote the letter?" I ask, in disbelief.

"But you're so young! And you brought company? I can't believe you!" she asks, seeming to get angrier by the second.

"Hey! I am perfectly capable of doing things, and I trust Asher with my life!"

"So, you know each other?" Asher asks not that out of the blue.

I glance at him to see a confused look on his face.

"I bumped into her in town not too long ago," I explain in a rush, still very confused.

"Okay, okay. Sorry I got ticked off; it's just that I really, really need your help."

Interested, I turn back to her and ask, "And what exactly do you need help with?"

She looks hesitatingly at Asher.

"You can trust him," I assure her.

She straightens up and, with sudden confidence, says, "I can help you find whoever is behind the killings, but, in turn, I need your help." How did she know who is behind the deaths; who is she? "I'm aware that this is a lot of information to handle at once, but hopefully what I tell you now will clear some things up." She takes a deep breath and continues, "Have you ever heard of the Enchanters' Child?"

Dread seeps into me and I ask her, "You're not one of those people who believe in the Enchanters' Child as well, are you? It's just a fairytale. And how do you know of the deaths? And about us?"

Asher, quietly next to me, says, "Let her finish."

I press my lips into a thin line and nod.

"No, not a fairytale. Believe me, I know."

"And how exactly are you so sure?" I ask her.

A look of severe caution crosses her face before she takes a deep breath. "Because the Enchanters' Child and I are one and the same."

I hear a sharp intake of breath from Asher, and I shake my head disbelievingly. "That's impossible," I tell her. "Magic and the sort don't exist."

"How are you so sure? I'm living proof that it does exist."

Seeing the skeptical look on my face, she sighs in frustration. Then she points at a dead flower on the stone floor of the gazebo and tells us, "Watch." As we watch the flower, it's slowly lifted off the ground. Gradually, it changes color, and within moments, in its place is a flower that looks like it has been freshly plucked from the earth. Tenderly, the flower floats back to the ground and Wren wipes her hands on skirt as if they're tainted before looking at us expectantly. I can feel the blood rushing from my face as I slowly back away, shaking my head.

I look up from the flower and see that Asher is staring in shock as well. He recovers faster than me, however. "Well this is something you don't see every day, and because no one else is speaking, I want to take this moment to just say that I was right. She is real," he declares, looking at me expectantly. "Well, are you done freaking out now, Zayne?"

I take another breath. Part of me is jealous of his ability to stay calm through anything.

In an attempt to steady myself, I ask her, "What I still

don't understand is what this has to do with your needing my help."

"I need to know what information you have gathered with your group that can help me."

"I don't know exactly what you're looking for."

"I was wondering if you had any leads on the whereabouts of whoever is behind the deaths you've been tracking."

Alarmed, Asher and I share a look before I ask," How do you about the deaths?"

"The Gavreel Society. It was formed by the Kingdom of Elrea, correct?"

Once I give a hesitant nod confirming her, she continues. "My father used to have ties with people in high positions there. It was his idea to have the Gavreel Society to be initiated if anything…unusual started happening and he's not around."

I raise my eyebrows in disbelief. "Is that how you knew how to find us?"

"It is." She says with a small smile.

"Why do you want to find who's causing these deaths?" Asher asks, cautious.

A look of concealed anger and grief flick over her face. "Because they killed my parents."

There is a brief pause of shocked silence before a slow understanding dawns on me. "You're saying that the Dark Sorcerer is the one who's behind these deaths?" I ask, recalling the story.

"I know it is. My parents left documents in my house

stating as such. These deaths have been happening long before now but they're just more frequent now."

A slow chill races down my back at the implication of it all. "And you just believe you can take care of this by yourself?"

Wren opens her mouth and then quickly closes it before blinking. "Yes." She says slowly.

"I'm afraid we don't have any information as of now that can help you." I say begrudgingly but quickly continue when I see her face fall. "However, I'll look at our records again tonight and see if I can find anything... under one condition."

Her face falls from the brief hope and a look of caution enters her eyes. "What?"

"If we find a lead then I come with you to find whoever it is. You're not the only one with a score to settle. Most of my life revolves around this Society."

Wren takes a slow breath in and looks at the ground. A few minutes tick by before she lets it out and looks at me. "Okay. I could use the help anyway."

Relief lets my shoulders sag. "Okay." I reply.

Wren slowly gets up and starts to make her way out of the garden when I call her again. "Wren."

She looks back with a glimmer of hope.

"Meet me at the bookstore tomorrow morning. There might be something there that can help us."

She gives a small nod and disappears into the night.

CHAPTER 6

QUINN

I BREATHE SLOWLY AS I nock the arrow on the string.
Sweat begins to trickle down my forehead as I aim
for the makeshift target I established behind Silas'
house. It was near sunrise when I had finally arrived in the
town that Damien had reported the Enchanters' Child
is most likely at. Silas' house is one of the safe houses
and lodgings for assassins and is the one stationed at this
town. Because Damien had announced my arrival under
the name 'Black Assassin', I have been required to wear
my mask while I'm around him. The whole thing is a
hassle because many assassins under Damien know my
face and that I'm an assassin at the compound. Just not
the infamous Black Assassin. I release the string and the
arrow shoots to the edge of the bull's eye. The mask isn't
helping my aim. Sighing, I gently put the bow on the
grass and sit down.

As much as I don't want to admit it, Silas was right.

The blacksmith's forge wagon had some of the best crafted weapons I've seen. And that girl. The way she held the dagger, she looked as though she knew what she was doing. But a girl, handling weapons? She must have wanted to buy it for a friend.

I'm off my game. I still don't have any leads on finding the Enchanters' Child. I lay on my back for a couple of minutes, enjoying the quiet that I don't experience very often. A thought comes to my mind and I sit up quickly. The bookstore. It might have something on the Enchanters' Child. Maybe the fairytale provides a clue. I stand up and wipe the dirt from my pants. As I walk to the stables to retrieve my horse, I see Hadrien.

"Have you had the chance to visit your Ma, Hadrien?" I ask him.

He shakes his head. "No, Master Silas only lets me go once every two months."

I smile as I notice he didn't call me 'sir.'

At that moment, Silas walks in and I tell him, "I'm taking Hadrien to help me with some errands."

I wasn't about to ask him for permission, but Hadrien is his servant. And I wasn't lying to the girl at the forge wagon; I have done so much wrong in my life by being an assassin, I like to believe there's still a little humanity left in me.

He looks at me and then Hadrien. "Very well."

I glance to Hadrien and see that his eyes are the size of saucers. I smile and motion for him to follow me.

"Do you know where your mother works?" I ask Hadrien.

Still looking confused and shocked, he stutters, "We-we're going to go see my mother?"

"Yes, I don't actually have an errand. I want you to have a chance to see her.

He grins and pours out thanks as he leads me through the streets to the seamstress' shop. "I work at Silas' house because Ma and I don't have much money and Silas pays a decent amount," he explains as he hurries along.

I smile at his enthusiasm and soon find myself standing before a quaint little shop where Hadrien rushes inside, so I follow him. Within, it smells like peppermint and the temperature is cool. There are fabrics on shelves all around the room and the wooden floor is clean.

"Ma!" Hadrien shouts and I watch as he rushes to a woman behind the counter.

Shock registers on her face, and a tear slips from her eye as she says, "Hadrien?" She laughs and kneels down to hug him. After they embrace, she pulls back. As if a thought has suddenly occurred to her, she asks, "What are you doing here?"

Hadrien grins and points at me, explaining, "He's Master Silas' friend! He said he could take me to see you."

Hadrien's mom looks at me with distrust but says, "Thank you."

I cringe. I hate when people look at me like that - like I'm no different from everyone else who is rich, and the mask doesn't help. If they only understood that I knew what it felt like.

After Hadrien had some more time to catch up with his

mother, I take him back to Silas' house and then head to the bookstore. I stop at an empty alley and quickly take off my mask. Once I check to ensure that nobody has noticed, I continue to the bookstore.

The bookstore is a small establishment just a little beyond Silas' house, but far enough away that the poor entered just as much as the rich did. I open the creaky door and am greeted with the smell of freshly printed pages and ink. As I step, the floorboards creak and I see a black staircase leading to the shelves upstairs. Having no clue where to begin, I walk up the staircase and remember that Damien had mentioned something about the Sorcerer wanting to find the Enchanters' Child first, and how the Enchanters' Child is known as a fairytale.

After searching for a couple of minutes, I finally discover where the fairytale books are kept. I kneel down and, after examining the shelf carefully, at last find a book on the Enchanters' Child. As I pull it, I notice that the cover is a dark blue and has gold lettering on it, stating: 'The Forgotten Gift.' As I flip through the pages, I rest on one talking about the Sorcerer.

The line was short, but it was enough. The Sorcerer lived in the Forest of Alberich. That place isn't on any maps you can find, and the only reason I know of it is because when my parents were alive, they had old maps passed down by their ancestors. Even when I was little, I was awed by the numerous old lands.

I gently return the book to its shelf and walk to the other side where all the maps are kept. As I move, I hear voices approaching me. Ignoring them, I reach out and pull free a map. I sit down on the wood floor and spread it open. The shelf is facing the wall, so unless someone came to look at the maps, I am hidden from view.

Once again, I hear voices as some people make their way to the other side of the shelf, where I had been just moments ago. Tuning their voices out, I scan the map and my eyes land on the empty space between the Kingdom of Elrea and the mountains of Orza. That is where the hidden forest is. I rub my eyes in frustration. That is a week's journey, even more. This location is the only thing that is hinted in the book. The forest is my only lead, and I'm not even sure if the Enchanters' Child is there – but if the Sorcerer already has her, then that's where she is. As I roll up the map, I stand. I'll buy the map in case I need it later. I'm about to step away when I hear something that makes me pause. I focus on the voices beyond the shelf.

"Are you sure this is safe?" It's a feminine voice – and it sounds familiar.

"Pretty sure; the bookstore is usually empty at this hour and nobody comes back here that often to get a fairytale," a male's voice responds.

The girl sighs and, after a pause, says, "Okay, but just in case, let's finish this quickly."

I breathe slowly and lean over to better hear them.

"Look for 'The Forgotten Gift'," the girl with the familiar voice tells the guy.

I jerk back in surprise, and there are a few moments of silence before the male says, "Found it."

Maybe they were just a couple of people wanting to buy a fairytale for a child. Maybe I'm overthinking this, but my years of training remind me to not jump to conclusions. Though, it is an odd coincidence.

There are continued moments of silence as I hear the gentle turn of pages. The man grunts in frustrations after a couple more minutes and says, "There's nothing here!"

Blood drains from my face as my previous conclusion is dismissed. These people aren't just here to buy the fairytale. They are looking for something. Just like I am.

"Here!" the girl exclaims and she reads out the line, "The Sorcerer lived in the Forest of Alberich, but the location is hidden and kept a secret."

"Well, that's something, but it doesn't help us. We don't know where that is," the male says.

I walk around the shelf quietly, eager to see the faces behind the voices. And then something that has not happened to me in a long time happens: the floorboard creaked. I whip my head up to see the girl and guy looking at me with wide eyes. Knowing that it was too late now, and deciding to act like I didn't hear them, I step out of the shadows and they simultaneously leap to their feet.

"Hello. Just here for a book," I tell them as I reach blindly for one. I pull the book out and when I look down at the title, I groan inside, seeing it's fairytale about some princess. I look back up and I see that they don't believe me. As my eyes scan more carefully over the female, I remember where I've heard her voice. It was the beautiful girl from the forge wagon.

"Hey, I know you. You're the guy from the forge wagon," the girl says, echoing my thoughts.

"Well, I hope you are not too attached. He heard us.

I could kill him if you want me to," the male says as his green eyes narrow at me.

In disbelief I say, "You're kidding, right?" These people are crazy. They have no idea who I am.

CHAPTER 7

WREN

ALARMED, I HALT Zayne from stepping toward the man. "Zayne, we're not killing anyone."

"Are you sure? Because that's the easiest way. I know a few places we could hide a body."

I glance at the man I'd met at the forge wagon and almost laugh at the expression on his face. He probably thought we were crazy. And Zayne's earlier comment scares me. I look at him. "No, there're other ways to solve this." I wrack my brain. "I could wipe his memory. Maybe if I hit his head hard enough, he'll forget about this." I was only half joking at this point. I didn't want to ruin his pretty face.

"What?" the man says in distress, but as I look closely, I can see that he isn't actually afraid - just alarmed.

I turn to Zayne and whisper, "What should we do?"

Zayne tears his gaze from the man and slowly focuses on me. "What?"

"I said, what should we do?"

Zayne shakes his head. "I don't know."

As we turn to the man, I'm about to speak, but he surprises me by asking, "You're looking for the Sorcerer?"

I stay silent and I think I see a calculating look in his eyes before he continues, hesitantly:

"I can use your help. I'm looking for him too."

I cautiously ask him, "Why?"

He gulps and looks me right in the eyes. "He killed my parents."

Immediately I start to feel a connection, but something about him is still bugging me. "He killed mine too," I say gently. "And I- I think he killed my aunt as well."

"You think?" asks Zayne softly.

"She was attacked by people made of shadow. Who else could it be?"

"Is that why you want to find the Sorcerer?"

There's a brief silence before he adds, "I can help you find the Forest of Alberich."

I take a sharp breath in. "How?"

I see him pause and then he tells us, "My parents. They had some old maps in the house that were passed down from our ancestors. Often, they would show them to me."

I swallow hard and turn to Zayne. "What do you think?" I ask him, wanting advice.

"The choice is yours, Wren. I already know my opinion isn't going to stop your decision." He was right, but I can see the distrust in his eyes as he peruses the man.

I turn to the man and I ask him, "What's your name?"

"Quinn."

"Well, Quinn, I'm Wren and this is Zayne. If you want, you can join us, but I'm letting you know that it's dangerous."

A dry laugh passes through his lips as he asks me, "You think I don't know that?"

I hear Zayne sigh behind me, and I tell Quinn, "We start in two days' time to collect what we need, that should be enough time. The longer it takes, the more deaths occur."

Okay, this was going to be something, and hopefully I didn't just make a huge mistake.

After Quinn walks past us and leaves, I look at Zayne. "I couldn't tell him no."

"I know; let's just hope he doesn't get killed in the process," Zayne says, sighing as he rubs his eyebrows with his ring finger and thumb.

I nod, but I have a feeling that Quinn is fully capable of surviving on his own, and what I am worried about is if I can trust both Quinn and Zayne, but I can't do this without them.

After we leave the bookstore and go our separate ways, I decide to go back to the inn and start getting ready for the journey. As I walk to the inn, I feel a small tug on my tattered gown. I look down to see a smiling child wearing a bright dress with flowers in her hair beaming up at me, and I smile, surprised, as she hands me one of the many roses in her little grip. As soon as I take the flower, she scurries back to her mother, who, as I look up see, is a woman who appears well-off when it came to money.

I smile at her and she smiles in return as the child darts back to her. This is why I love Trading Day. It is one of the few times when the gap between castes blurs and everyone is each other's equal.

I walk the rest of the way to the inn; Zayne said he wanted to go buy some things for the journey, so he didn't walk back with me. I think I have everything, but if I need anything, I'll buy it later. Right now, however, I am too exhausted to do anything else but sleep.

CHAPTER 8

ZAYNE

DESPITE THE CIRCUMSTANCES, I feel excitement. I am finally doing something, rather than sitting around. I walk to Asher's house and knock. There are a few moments of silence and then he opens the door.

"Nice to see you again," Asher says, looking at me, and then he pushes the door farther open and lets me in.

"What's up?" he asks as we both walk into the sitting room.

I crash onto the couch in exhaustion. "I'm leaving for a while. The girl, Wren, and I think we have a lead, but it's not a strong one," I tell him as I close my eyes.

There's a moment of silence and I look to see Asher staring at me. He says with determination, "I'm coming with you."

"No," I say immediately.

He sighs in frustration and asks, "Why not?"

"I need someone here to watch the group. And, Asher?"

"Yeah?"

"Don't tell anyone about this. Even the Gavreel Society. I don't want them to be too hopeful on a bad lead, and I want to keep this quiet for now. Just tell them that I went somewhere on an errand and won't be back for some time."

Asher sighs, knowing that I am right. I need him here. He reluctantly agrees and we walk together back to the door. "Zayne?" I turn toward him and he looks me straight in the eye. "Don't die."

"I'll try." To be honest, I am scared. I give him a smile, but I know he can see through it. I don't say goodbye because I don't believe in them. Saying goodbye is like saying that there's a chance I might never see him again.

There are more and more people arriving in town because of the Autumn Celebration. Why the kingdoms hold a festival that lasts a week is lost to me. Games are being set up for the start of the Autumn Celebration, and I feel a wave of sadness when I realize I won't be there to experience them. It is one of my favorite times of the year, but there are more pressing issues than celebrating. The journey ahead reminds of the guy that we met in the bookstore. I hope Wren made the right decision when she let him join us. We can't have him slowing us down.

The next few days pass in a blur and, before I know it, it's time. As I ride down the streets on my horse with my things, I take in all that makes this town what it is. It isn't much, but I'm going to miss the sound of children laughing, the vibrant colors, the voices of people around me, and so much more. I love this place and I feel a tinge of sadness as I realize that I didn't get to spend much time here. I am going to miss the Gavreel Society and especially Asher. They are the people that I trust the most in the world, the people I have grown up with.

As I look around, I realize that more people have arrived in the town; the streets are more crowded than usual. Around me, games are arranged for many ages, from children to grown men. I have to help these people. It's my duty. If we don't do anything, then what other hope do they have?

As I reach the gates, I see two smaller figures in the distance, and as I near them, I realize its Wren and Quinn. They both carry satchels similar to mine and have determined looks on their faces. They both have horses; we all decided that walking there is out of the question - it is too far. I look around; we all have reasons for doing this. For Wren and Quinn, it's their parents. I can't imagine what they have gone through, but hopefully what we're doing will stop what happened to them - whatever happened to each victim of the Sorcerer.

CHAPTER 9

QUINN

WHAT I TOLD Wren isn't exactly a lie. I do think that the Sorcerer killed my parents. Who else could it have been? Yet, I still feel a bit of guilt for lying to her. Nonetheless, I have to do what I have to do. I'm tired of doing what Damien asks me to. I want to be what I desire, and I don't want someone else choosing my actions in life. And, technically, I wasn't telling Wren or Zayne anything that will hurt them. All I have to accomplish is finding the Enchanters' Child, and I'm helping them in the process.

Wren pulls me out of my thoughts when she says, "We should get going."

I take a deep breath and, at once, we all turn toward the road ahead of us. Whatever we do now, we can't go back. I just hope with all my heart that this works.

The guards don't check our bags because we are leaving the city, not entering it, and soon we are beyond the gates. Disbelief strikes me as I realize that we're actually doing this. I adjust my satchel and, together, we all ride out. In the beginning, it will be easy. I am more worried about crossing the other kingdoms. The closer we get to the Forest of Alberich, the more the Sorcerer's magic has its affect.

Wren and Zayne follow me, and after a couple hours of riding, I hear a voice call out. I turn around and see that it's Wren. She gestures for Zayne and I to follow her to the side of the road. By this time, the sun has come up and I feel it beat against my back as Wren turns to both of us.

She looks at us gravely. "The book says that there's an invisible barrier around the forest and that the only way to pass it is to use the Lochaere, the sacred blue stone that let the Enchanters get through. That's the first step. What we need to get before going any further."

I nod at her, having memorized the book at this point, searching for any answers. "The book said the Lochaere is in the Kingdom of Elrea."

"What?" Zayne says, and as I look at him, I see that his face has gone white.

"Are you alright?" Wren asks in concern.

Zayne shakes his head and says, "I'm fine, it's just that- isn't that far away?"

"Yes, which is why we have to make haste and stop as little as possible," I tell him slowly.

He nods and the look of disbelief is gone as quickly as it came.

Wren, after a pause, continues, "That means we have to stop by the kingdom."

In confusion, I ask her, "But how can we find the stone? It can be anywhere in the kingdom."

She glances at Zayne quickly and then looks at me. "I have my ways."

I frown. "Like what?"

She glances at me before looking at the ground. "I spent a lot of time in Elrea when I was little and I think there are places I can narrow down our search to."

Watching her face, I know that she isn't telling me the whole truth and I put this information in the back of my head, knowing that she isn't willing to confess the real reason at this moment.

After a small pause, Wren quickly glances at Zayne before asking me, "How long do you think it will take us to make it to Elrea?"

"Around five days."

She sighs and says, "Alright, that's a plan and we can work on it during the journey there. Five days is a deadline and we can't waste time."

Zayne remains quiet and nods. We start walking again and I warn them, "Careful. The closer we get to the Forests of Alberich, the further we are entering into the Sorcerer's territory."

The rest of the day goes by quickly enough and we ride until we are too tired to continue. By this time, it's late evening and the sky is a shade of purple with pink and orange hues. We settle into a small clearing off the path which Zayne had spotted and I sit, leaning on a tree after I tie my horse. Soon, Wren and Zayne join me. They sit on the grass, and as they are taking their satchels off their backs, we hear a rustling noise in the trees above us. All at once, we look up. I force down the urge to gasp as I see a set of brown eyes staring right back down at us. As soon as it was there, though, it's gone.

"Tree people," I say to no one in particular.

"What?" Wren asks.

"Tree people," I repeat again. "Across the forest there are small villages and we call them tree people, you know, because they travel by tree?" I encourage. But by the look on their faces, they have no idea what I'm talking about and are terrified. My shoulders droop and I sound perplexed when I ask them, "Seriously? You didn't know that?"

I guess the tree people are one of the many things people around here don't know about, but I do, because there are many where I used to live. There are thousands of them, and yet here they have no idea what I'm talking about and instead stare at me blankly.

Zayne snaps out of it first and asks, "Will they cause us trouble?"

I, still baffled, ask, "How do you not know who they are?"

"Answer the question," Zayne says in return.

I stare at him for a few seconds and then say, "No. Tree people aren't known for their violence unless you get on their bad side." They both visibly relax, and I would have laughed if it wasn't for the look of seriousness on their faces.

CHAPTER 10

WREN

WE TOOK TURNS watching that night. The moon pierces the darkness and thousands of stars twinkle as I sit on a log while Zayne and Quinn sleep. Looking closely at their breathing patterns, however, I can see that they aren't asleep, but instead lie quietly surrounded by their thoughts. I am wrapped in my own thoughts as well.

When we get to the Kingdom of Elrea, I can use a locating spell to find the Lochaere. The only way to summon a locating spell is to have a piece of whatever I want to find with me, but what Zayne and Quinn don't know is that the small blue stone hanging from the necklace Aunt Adnis gave me is actually a piece of the Lochaere. That's another secret I can't tell anyone. It's the one thing that gives me leverage and these two already know more about me than anybody. The only problem is that the necklace has to be close enough to the stone for it to work. When we are close enough to the stone, I should feel a tug. The plan is shaky at best, but it will have to do for now.

I feel a hand on my shoulder and look up to see Quinn. I jolt, surprised by how I hadn't noticed him approaching. His blue eyes hold the same look of loss and a thousand nights of bad dreams as mine, and my heart aches for him. He gives me a small smile and says, "I can take watch now."

I look at him, confused. "I just started thirty minutes ago, and besides, I can't sleep," I say, shrugging.

Instead of leaving, he sits next to me on the log and sighs. I feel butterflies at the closeness. "The nightmares never go away, do they?" It wasn't a question but more of a statement.

I laugh dryly. "No."

Staring at the trees on the other side of the clearing, he says, "Most of the time, to keep my mind off it during the day, I run and I focus on the pain. I push myself until I can't think about anything but the pain. But during the night, nothing is stopping the thoughts from flooding in."

I say nothing, but it scares me how much I can relate. We fall into a comfortable silence as we look out at the moon and stars. In that moment, I feel closer to him than I have with anyone else before.

The next morning, we pack up quickly and once again start riding with Quinn as the lead. It's unusual, having someone else leading you. My entire life, I was the one leading and the one in control, but just this once, I have no choice but to give up control. It has me on edge, but I would be lying to say that a small part of me wasn't relieved. Zayne and I stay close to him as we make our way down the path.

I have a knife in my boot and a second one up my sleeve, and I don't doubt that the others have something on them as well. Before we had started this morning, I watched Quinn move and I see a cat-like grace about him. When standing, his feet swiftly pace as if he is gliding. There is more to him than he lets on. It is in the way he holds himself, the way he talks as if he can't trust anyone, and the way he moves. But I'm not going to push it, because, like him, I have secrets too. While I do believe it's important that we trust each other, it doesn't mean I am about to tell them everything.

Suddenly, I glimpse something at the corner of my vision. A blur of black. At first, I dismiss it as a trick of light, but then I see it again. I stop and motion for Zayne and Quinn to halt as well. They give me questioning looks, but do as I say. I remain still and search the trees. I see another blur of black at the corner of my sight, and I whirl around to find myself staring directly into the eyes of- of… well, I don't actually know what it is. It's black with four legs and razor-sharp claws. Its red eyes watch us as a predator would watch its prey. Frightened, my horse bucks under me and I quickly dismount to avoid getting hurt. Zayne and Quinn quickly do the same as they slip out their daggers.

No one says a word, but that is when I notice a faint purple symbol on the shoulder of the creature. A symbol that has haunted me wherever I go. The sign of the Sorcerer. He found us.

All the questions disappear from my mind as I focus on the task at hand. Staying alive. I reach into my sleeve and pull out my dagger. Swinging my arm back, I aim at its heart and hold my breath as the dagger soars through the air - just to strike and then rebound from its impact on the creature. This is going to be a problem. As if my dagger was a trigger, the creature charges toward me like a battering ram. I roll away just seconds before it can hit me.

"It must have a weak spot!" Quinn shouts.

The trouble is finding it. It can be anywhere.

The creature turns in the direction I moved, but before it can attack me again, Zayne's dagger hits the side of the creature. The result is the same: no damage. *How do we kill it, how do we kill it?* The question repeats in my mind.

A thought springs up, and I hesitate for half a second before reaching into my boot and grabbing the second dagger. I rise to see that the creature is approaching Zayne with its back to me. I look at the ground in haste and catch sight of a rock the size of my palm. I throw it at the creature, where it strikes and then pings off its back. It swings toward me, completely forgetting about Zayne. All my surroundings disappear as I focus on my mark. I throw the dagger and it sinks right into the purple symbol on the creature's shoulder. At once, it screams a chilling sound exactly like a human's and then turns into black ash, disappearing.

I slump in relief.

Quinn looks at me in concern, but when he realizes

I'm okay, he asks, "How'd you know that was going to work?"

"I didn't."

"What the bloody hell was that?" Zayne asks.

"I don't know, but it's the Sorcerer's doing," I say.

"What?" Quinn says, and I can hear the disbelief in his voice. "How?"

"Remember the purple mark on the shoulder? That's the Sorcerer's sign," I say.

"He must know what we're doing. Somehow," Zayne says.

"He found us so soon," I mutter. "And this is barely the beginning. He knows about us and he's going to conjure up more dangerous creatures. Ones that are faster, smarter, and stronger. We have to keep our eyes open," I say louder as I start to make my way to where I had left my horse but when I turn to look for it, it isn't there. None of the horses are. They must have bolted during the fight. Frowning, I look at Zayne and Quinn. We must go on foot.

The rest of the day, we move in caution now that we know the Sorcerer is after us. When the other two aren't looking, I put up some protection wards around us so that if something dangerous is approaching, I will know. Another tense night passes during which no one sleeps, and in the morning, Quinn tells us disturbing news.

"We have to go off the path if we're ever going to make it," he explains.

Unease spreads through me as we leave the safety of our road but it's necessary. Pine needles hide any footsteps, and soft light filters through the leaves to greet us. The scenery is like a switch, the path a stark contrast to the forest. Birds chirp and creatures scurry around. I let out a soft laugh. It is like a fairytale after all.

CHAPTER 11

ZAYNE

DISCOMFORT COURSES THROUGH me as we walk. The book said the Lochaere is in the Kingdom of Elrea. What if the other two find out who I am? They couldn't; no one knows except the royal family and high advisors. My identity being a secret is the only way I'm able to do any of this. I put the thought at the back of my mind so I can return to it later. There's nothing I can do about it now.

Suddenly, Wren hisses in pain and crumbles to the ground, clutching her head. Alarmed, I shout at Quinn to stop and kneel down in a rush to see if she's okay. A small voice at the back of my mind whispers: of course she isn't. I shake it away and check her pulse. It's weak but it's there. I let out a sigh of relief and smile. I try to tell myself I'm only worried so much because without her we can't do anything… but I know that isn't it. I hear hurried footsteps and look up to see Quinn.

"Is she alright?" he asks with genuine concern.

"She's alive," I tell him.

He reaches into his satchel and pulls out his water skin. "Here, give her some water."

I reach out and take it while gently pulling Wren into a sitting position, making her drink some. Automatically she gulps it down and her eyes flutter open.

"Can you stand?" I ask her softly, after a degree of color returns to her face.

She gives a weak nod and I help her up. When I'm sure she can support her weight without collapsing on her face, I let her go.

"What happened?" Quinn asks.

She frowns slightly and winces at the memory. "I'm not sure, actually. I felt a sharp pain in my head that hurt like nothing I have ever experienced. It felt like it was eating at me."

I furrow my brows, pondering what she said. It was odd for a headache to come so suddenly and with that much pain.

"You think you can walk now?" Quinn asks her.

She nods. "Yes, it's almost gone."

As we are walking, I hang back with Wren – out of hearing range from Quinn – and ask her, "Could it be something to do with the Sorcerer and who you are?"

Her face pales drastically. "I didn't think about that." She swallows. "Whoever it is could have found a way to target me specifically."

I squeeze her hand in reassurance and then release it. "Let's hope it doesn't happen again."

She smiles weakly and then we increase our pace to catch up with Quinn. He pushes a branch out of the way and then stops abruptly. I halt myself from crashing into him just in time. "What is it?" I inquire, concerned. His shoulders are taut and full of tension.

"I'm pretty sure we already passed this broken tree," he says cautiously, slowly. The tree in question was broken in half, situated next to a mossy rock.

"Are you sure?" Wren asks in concern.

"I thought you said you knew what you are doing," I growl.

"I do," he snaps. "I've never lost my way before."

Wren bites her lip in worry. "In the worst-case scenario, the Sorcerer could have used this 'adrift' spell, where it causes the victims to be lost for hours on end."

"This guy isn't going to give us a moment of respite, is he?" Quinn says. No one replies, because we all know the answer.

"What are we going to do now?" Zayne asks.

"Well, the best thing right now is to be on the move. Staying in one place isn't good, and hopefully we'll find a village or town that will help us," Quinn declares.

Wren nods. "That's a good idea and our best option."

We walk for hours. Before I know it, another day passes.

Our food and water start to run out after five days, and true panic sets in. We have to find a settlement with people.

On the sixth day, we find a lake, but disappointment sets in as we discover it's too dirty to drink from. Exhaustion creeps in and pain in my stomach conquers any other thought. Taking a glance at the others, I see that they're in the same condition. We are dirty, tired, hungry, and it comes to a point where we don't think we can go any farther.

Just as I think I can't go on, I feel a sharp jab at my side. It's Wren. Through cracked lips, she points ahead with excitement and says, "Look!"

I swivel my attention forward to see a town in the distance. I close my eyes and then open them. It's still there. *Please don't be a mirage.*

Together, we stumble toward what we hope is a refuge - with people who can help us.

CHAPTER 12

QUINN

THE JOY OF seeing a town is mixed with caution as we grow nearer to the settlement. We don't want them to think we are dangerous. But, as I remember the conditions we are in, I know we have no other chance. As we approach the town, I realize it is smaller than I originally thought. Because the only settlement with gates is one at the heart of the kingdom, there are no guards as we enter.

The town is like a fairy land, with flowers and many people laughing and walking around. In all the commotion, no one takes note of the three strangers looking as if they'd been to hell and back. Zayne gestures to us and I see him point at a tavern doubling as an inn. The building is no different from the rest of town. There are flowers adorning the walls and ivy crawling up the side of it. The wood appears brand new, and both light and laughter shine from within.

We enter the tavern and I notice that the inside also mirrors the rest of town. Flowers hang on the walls and are placed in vases at the center of each table. The people within are quite different from any I have ever seen. They hardly seem the type who will start tavern brawls or pick our pockets. They are wearing bright clothes and there are even women with flowers in their hair.

But looks can always be deceiving, so I keep my guard up as we enter. I immediately tense when I realize everyone is staring at us. Our dirty, tattered clothes are a far cry from their garbs. While avoiding eye contact, we make our way to the bar doubling as a reception desk.

The man behind the counter is hefty and completely throws me off when he smiles. Immediately, like it was a trigger, everything goes back to normal and people start talking once more, like nothing had happened. An eerie feeling washes over me, but I brush it off.

"Do you have a room?"

The man shrugs. "Sure, if you can pay for it."

We all exchange an uneasy glance. "That's the thing. We don't have any money," Wren says. The man starts shaking his head, but Wren rushes on, "We can work it off."

The man once again shakes his head. "I'm not short any hands and I don't need anyone else working for me." He shrugs. He sees our desperate looks and sympathy is shown in his eyes. "I'm sorry."

We dejectedly thank him and move to the side as someone else steps up to the counter.

"What are we going to do?" Zayne asks.

Wren sighs. "I have no idea."

A calm, deep voice interjects, "Excuse me?"

We all whirl around to see a man, aged somewhere in his fifties with gray hair, smiling at us.

"I couldn't help but overhear your problem."

Oh great.

"And?" Zayne asks him with slight irritation.

The man shows no reaction to his tone and continues, "I have a place you can stay. My wife and I own a barn on our property that we're not using."

"Why are you willing to help us?" I ask suspiciously.

The man gives a broad smile and says, "I don't know where you folks are from, but here we help others because it's the nice thing to do."

Kill me now. All this color and happy goodness is making me sick. Something isn't right.

"We can't possibly intrude," Wren says with a shake of her head.

The man waves it away and sticks out a hand, and as Zayne shakes it, he says, "My name is Mark Bennett."

When none of us gives our names, he coughs uncomfortably and motions for us to follow him out of the tavern. Wren's stomach grumbles and she smiles sheepishly.

"You guys must be starving. Lucky for you, my wife is always cooking something or the other," Mark says and then adds, "You all should probably take a bath too."

We arrive at a house in no time. The building is half-timbered with tiles on the roof and a pair of chimneys. It's divided into two floors, and I see the barn peeking out from behind it.

"You all can go ahead to the barn. I'll call down the servants to pull baths for you and bring over some food."

As we walk toward the barn, I can't ignore this weird feeling I've been experiencing. "Something doesn't feel right," I tell the others.

"What do you mean?" Zayne asks, drawing his eyebrows together.

"I did feel strange walking into the town, but I think that's just because we don't know these people," Wren adds.

I frown. "Yeah, that's probably it."

We arrive at the barn, and I note it as small and quaint from the outside. Though abandoned, there is something calm about the place.

"Why do they have a barn to begin with?" Zayne mutters.

"I don't know, but I'm not about to start complaining," Wren replies.

As we enter the tall structure, I realize to my surprise that the barn is less of a barn and more of a small home. There aren't even animals within. The ground floor has a small corridor lined with chairs and doors leading to other rooms. Usually barns aren't like this, but this town is odd, so I'm not going to ask about it and push it further. There is a ladder extending to the second floor, and when I climb up, I find that this section resembles more of a barn, with fresh hay and a small window looking out to the Bennetts' house.

Zayne and Wren meet me on the second floor moments later. After surveying the area, I pull out the thin blankets we packed for the trip and lay them on top of the hay. I hear a dull knock on the wooden door below. I wipe the hay off my pants as I rise and descend the stairs.

When I open the door, a servant greets me with a platter of food including fruits and cheese and a pouch of money, which she explains the Bennetts have given us to spend in town. My mouth waters and I open the entrance wider to let her in. She brings the food upstairs and leaves without another word. Zayne and Wren's expressions mirror mine when they see the meal.

After eating quickly, exhaustion takes over, and as I fall asleep, I can't help but think that something isn't right.

CHAPTER 13

WREN

AFTER I TAKE a bath, I slip out to uncover more about this town. With Quinn sleeping and Zayne checking out the maps to try and decipher our location, no one notices. Just in case, before I leave, I whisper a spell. To everyone looking at me, instead of seeing the young woman who had stumbled in that same morning with two others looking just as bad as her, they see a young man with brown hair and green eyes, who had not a care in the world. I change my walk to match one of a boy's, as lighthearted as the rest of the townies. In addition, I cast a separate spell to deepen my voice.

By this time, it is late evening and many people are milling around. Every single person seems to be smiling and showing a bunch of happiness. I would be lying to say it isn't unnerving. People I have never seen before wave at me and smile. Yet, if anyone truly recognizes me - or if there is a secret beneath the surface of this town -

I'm going to find out. I decide to start at the taverns. It is a good thing I cast the impersonating spell when I left, so no one will find it suspicious that a female is visiting multiple pubs alone.

The first one I enter is a pub called, 'The Twin Moons.' As soon as I walk in, I'm not surprised to find it mirrors the inn we had first stumbled upon. Where there should be drunken shouts and gambling and brawls, there is sobriety and polite chatter and quiet laughter. No one looks at me as I step in.

I frown; it all seems fake.

I journey through the crowd – which isn't very hard – to the bar. There is no one there except the bartender and a customer perched on a stool with a drink. I approach a matching stool and plop down.

The bartender walks toward me and smiles. "What would you like, miss?" he asks.

I give a small smile. "Just some water, please."

He nods and leaves to retrieve my order.

Suddenly, I freeze as his words register. *He called me 'miss.'*

I squint at the bartender, who seems oblivious to what just happened. I glance sideways at the other man sitting at the bar and see him looking down at his glass. From here, I can't tell if he heard anything or not, or if he can see I'm a girl as well. I tense as the bartender comes back to place the water in front of me, but he just walks away like nothing happened.

I gesture for the bartender and he comes back with a

bright smile. I give a cheery smile of my own and ask him, "How long have you worked here?"

His smile fades a little and his face goes blank, but, just like that, the grin is back and he asks, "What else would you like, miss?"

A chill runs down my spine and I jump out of the seat.

Exhaling slowly, I look around to see that no one in the pub has noticed anything. Suddenly, a man enters my vision and, with a start, I realize it's the guy that was sitting at the bar.

His words slur as he grabs my collar and says, "You. Leave. Now. Trap."

I remove his hands off my collar with a shake and a sense of alarm. He was obviously drunk, and I hurry out of the pub before he causes a scene.

Taking a deep breath outside, a sudden thought comes to mind and, with shaking hands, I whisper a quick unveiling spell. Immediately, the greenery and the flowers slowly fade, leaving dead foliage. The only indications of 'people' are shadows moving. All the bright colors around me dull significantly as they turn to murky colors. With a tremble, the spell fades away, and bright colors and flowers once again fill my vision. But when I look closer, I can see a glimmer indicating that it is all just an illusion. Sounds lower around me as I can hear my pulse beating in my ears. Understanding washes over me with horror.

I run.

I reach the "barn" in record time and open the oak door with a thud. Rushing to the top floor, relief washes over me as I find Quinn and Zayne. "We have to leave.

Now. It- it's all a trap," I say in a rush, still breathless from my run.

A silence follows and then Zayne grins widely. "No, I never want to leave," he says, like he's drunk.

A chill runs down my spine.

I turn to Quinn, to check if he is in the same state and, with panic, see that he has a drunken smile to match.

Quinn reaches for some more food from the plate and I watch in shock as his eyes glaze over even more as he pops the grapes in his mouth. Realization floods in with fear, and as Zayne reaches for some cheese, I knock it out of his hand. "No, don't eat the food!"

He pouts like a child and then anger begins setting in. "Don't tell me what to do," he spits out.

I back up. As he starts marching up to me in anger, I do the first thing that comes to mind. I stun him. His eyes grow wide as he realizes he can't move. After I do the same thing with Quinn, I suck in an unsteady breath.

An idea sparks in my head a few minutes later and I wonder why I haven't thought of it before. We could just leave. The small voice in my head tells me it can't be that easy, but I ignore it. Deciding that the poison has left them both, I break the spell I had put over them. They blink and, at the same time, let out loud groans of pain.

"What happened?" Quinn asks in confusion.

"Nothing," I say innocently. "You fell asleep."

"Did you learn anything?" Zayne asks me.

I pale. I tell them about the bartender.

"But just because he responded weird to your question-"

"Yeah, I don't understand why we have to leave because of that. We still have to rest up, and pack food and water for our journey. We can't just leave." Quinn argues,

I know by their expressions that they are not taking me seriously.

I try to show Zayne that there's more to it than what I am saying because he's the only one that knows about my magic, but he only grows more confused, scrunching his eyebrows together. Sighing, hoping I'm not making a mistake, I say, "I-" I clear my throat and continue, "I also d- did a spell and this town isn't exactly what it looks to be."

"Wait, what? For a second *I* thought you said you did a spell," Quinn says, releasing the 'l' with a smack.

I clear my throat again. "Yeah, because that's what I said."

He barks out a hard laugh. "You're joking. The only one who can do that is the-" He cuts off abruptly and shakes his head in an aggressive motion. "No, you can't be."

I gulp. Zayne and I watch him carefully.

Quinn's face is pale and a little green. I knew he was going to be shocked, but it almost looks as though he is disgusted. About what, I don't know. Me? I would be lying to say that the implication doesn't hurt.

Shifting his body to face Zayne, Quinn points at him but asks me, "And did he know?"

"Yes," Zayne says, but I ignore him and continue:

"But that's not important. This town...well, it isn't a town at all."

"What do you mean?" Zayne asks, confused.

"I did an unveiling spell, and I found out that this town isn't exactly what we see. The spell reveals things for what they really are. When I did the spell, all of the flowers and people faded away; there was just murk and shadows."

"So, what does this mean then?" Zayne asks.

I take a deep breath. "I think it means that this settlement is a conjuring of the Sorcerer."

"We thought we were safe, but in reality, we aren't safe at all," Zayne says as realization begins flooding in.

"Exactly," I say, nodding. "And we can't take the food with us or eat it either; it's poisonous and makes you want to stay here. That's why I had to put a stunning spell on both of you, because once I tried to stop you guys from eating the food, you were getting kind of mad." I grin. "You started getting mad over a piece of cheese."

Zayne scowls.

"Wait, what I don't understand is why you didn't get poisoned too. You ate the food," Quinn says, and some relief floods into me. Talking is a good sign.

I shrug. "I don't know. I guess it's because I'm a trained Arobol."

"You're what?" Zayne asks.

"It's what we call ourselves, humans that can do magic. There used to be many of us," I explain as sadness creeps into me.

"So, because you're..." Quinn trails off, trying to find the right word.

"Arobol."

"Right. You are immune?" Quinn finishes.

"Yes, I think so," I say.

"So, what are we going to do now?" Zayne asks me.

"I was sort of thinking that we can just waltz out," I explain sheepishly.

Zayne looks at me with contempt and Quinn as though I have just grown two heads.

"I think that is the stupidest thing I have ever heard in my life," Quinn finally says.

"Okay, I admit that it isn't the best of plans," I relent.

"That's the understatement of the year," Zayne snorts.

"It can't be that easy," Quinn adds.

I glare at them. "Glad to see you two actually agree on something."

"Yeah, it's not going to happen again," Zayne says, and Quinn nods in agreement.

I roll my eyes. "But what are we going to do?" I ask them.

We think in silence and then Zayne says, "I can go check if we can leave in the first place, which we probably can't. Then we can explore our options."

It's a shaky idea at most, but it's the best we've got.

CHAPTER 14
ZAYNE

As I walk through town and pass the various buildings and citizens, I can't help but ponder what Wren told me. Now that I think about it, as I look closely at the people, I can see that their moves are more mechanical than natural. I suppress a shudder and continue walking toward the edge of town. I stop cautiously when I near the border, gazing out at the forest in front of me.

I can only just distinguish where the forest ends and the town begins from a slight discoloration in the grass. Now that I consider it, this is a weird location for a town. There are no roads leading in or out.

I look around for something that I can throw and find a tiny stone. Swinging my arm back, I then fling the stone and hold my breath. The object sails over the border like nothing is there and my eyes go wide. *Maybe it really is that easy.* I walk to the edge and relax as I take a step out. For a second, nothing happens and relief floods through me.

But then almost immediately, I'm thrown backward. As I land, head cracking against the ground, I wince with pain. *Or maybe not.* I get up, brush the dirt off my pants, and look at the edge with dejection. What are we going to do?

The pain is already starting to fade, so I suck in a breath before forcing myself to start walking back to the barn. I'm halfway there when I'm stopped by a middle-aged woman. She has black hair, and her blue eyes squint up at me as she raises a basket filled with nuts into my view.

"Would you like some nuts?" she asks sweetly.

I frown. *Odd.* Then I remember what Wren told me about not eating any of the food and how these people aren't people. I kindly shake my head and move on, but not two minutes later, I'm stopped by another person offering me bread. It's like...

I pale. Like they want me to eat the food. Soon, there are people swarming me with offers of sustenance and drink. I run as fast as I can to the barn.

CHAPTER 15

QUINN

S HE IS THE Enchanters' Child. I can't believe it. This makes it so much harder, because now I actually, personally know her. But I have to give her over. Nothing, not even this, is anything compared to my freedom. Especially when my sister is at risk if I fail. I can't. I have to complete my mission.

But... I *can* put it off. I know Damien well enough to distrust him. So, to ensure that he will give me back my freedom, I'll find the Sorcerer while I'm at it. That will make sure that he keeps his word because I'm getting rid of the only person other than Wren that threatens his power. So, I won't capture Wren yet...

Yeah, that's what I tell myself. I still can't help but feel a little disgusted that this is the best I can be. I walk downstairs, looking for Wren. After Zayne left, Wren started reading through a book that she kept in her satchel. She mentioned something about her parents writing it for her. I can't believe that her parents were the famous Enchanters.

I find her in one of the rooms. It resembles a study and Wren is hunched over a desk with the book open in front of her. She tucks a piece of hair that escaped her braid behind her ear and looks up when I enter.

"Hey," she says, smiling.

I give a smile that hopefully doesn't look forced.

I must have showed something on my face, because she sighs and asks, "I hope this isn't too much. Knowing I'm the Enchanters' Child, I mean."

She mistakes my guilt for disbelief, and I sigh and sink into a chair. "Honestly? I was surprised at first, but so much has happened in my life that I'm past being surprised and reacting too much." Okay, that wasn't a lie. "So, what are you looking for?" I ask, pointing to the brown book in front of her.

"If we can't leave then I have to find a counter spell and, with a town of this size, it's going to have to be huge. If Zayne can't pass the border then that means there's some sort of shield around the town, so I'm looking for a spell on shields."

I shake my head. Despite the circumstances, I'm amazed and a little unsettled. If that power got into the wrong hands... *Like Damien*, a small voice at the back of my head says. I ignore it and, at that moment, Zayne barges into the room.

"Okay, well, I was right. There is a barrier," he says, out of breath.

"Are you alright?" Wren asks with concern.

"I was stopped on the way here. Multiple times. I think people here are trying to make us stay. They were offering me food."

"We should leave soon, then," Wren says. Then she frowns. "Maybe I can narrow my search if you describe it. Did you see anything unusual when you found the barrier?"

"I don't think so."

"Are you sure?" Wren pushes. "Any detail can be important."

"Well, the color of the grass is different on the other side of the barrier, and for some reason, a stone could pass when I couldn't." He shrugs. "But I don't know if that is any help."

"It might be," she says. "The stone can represent elements or non-living objects in general." She starts flipping through the pages.

"Hey, is there a chance you can take the spell off the food and water?" I ask her, a sudden idea coming to mind.

"Yes, I think so. It might take a while, though," she says without looking up from the book.

I sigh and leave the room. We still need some food and water to take with us when we leave. I exit the barn and walk to the main house. I shudder as I approach, remembering the people within aren't even real. I hesitate only for a second before I knock on the door, which opens after a few beats of silence. A servant stands there with a smile. I shake my head. She looks so real.

"Good evening," I say, greeting her.

"Good evening," she echoes.

"I was wondering if the Bennetts would kindly give us some more food."

She frowns. "Did we not give you some already, some time ago?"

I smile, hoping I look sheepish. "Well, yes. But we have had quite a long journey and are quite hungry."

"Very well, I will ask the Bennetts. Please, come in," she says, opening the door wider.

I walk in and the first thing that hits me is the quiet. The house is blanketed in pin-drop silence. As I look around, I realize that there are no pictures of the Bennett family - or of anything, for that matter. The servant leads me to a room and gestures for me to sit down before leaving. I take a seat on the couch and watch as the grandfather clock in the corner of the room ticks. The silence puts me on edge and makes my skin crawl. I look up to see Mark Bennett staring at me from the doorway and I jump.

I stop myself from bolting as he greets me with a nod. I look at his figure to see if there are any weapons. None, but I do notice him holding a basket in his hands.

"Did you guys settle in alright?" he asks kindly, but now it seems robotic.

"Yes, we feel right at home," I lie, wanting to leave.

"That is good to hear," he replies. He sees me eyeing the basket and laughs. "Oh yes. Here is the food." Maybe I am getting paranoid, but I think I saw his eyes glint when he said the word 'food.'

"Many thanks," I reply as I take the basket and move to quickly exit the house.

When the main house is well behind me, I break from my false calm and hurry to the "barn." I reach it and enter the room where I left Wren. Zayne is there with her, and when I approach, they both look up with concern.

"What?" I ask, confused.

"Did anything happen?" Wren asks.

They were concerned? About me? They can't be concerned about me. That means they are getting attached. I shake my head in a daze. "No, I'm not hurt."

They relax. "Oh, good," Wren says. I gulp.

"We were just discussing how we have to get to the Kingdom of Elrea. We think the best time to get the Lochaere is when there are a lot of people in the kingdom and the castle. The only time that happens is during the Autumn Celebration Ball. Zayne is apparently from that kingdom, so he can help us get around. This means we are on a time schedule."

"You're from the Kingdom of Elrea? Why didn't you say so earlier?" I ask Zayne, surprised.

He shrugs. "I didn't think it was important."

"Everything is important," Wren says, sighing. "But that's not what's important at the present moment. We have to get out of here first and then get to the kingdom on time."

"Okay, well, did you find the counter spell in the book?" I ask her.

"I think so; did you get the food?" she asks in return.

I lift the basket. "Right here."

CHAPTER 16
WREN

WE HAVE TO get out of here. This town is like a cage where the only escape is through the one door that landed you here in the first place. That is about to change. The first task, however, is that I lift whatever spell is present on the food. I open the basket that Quinn left on the table before he had gone with Zayne to give me some time alone to do the magic. Glancing in, I see there are also three canteens of water. I lay all the provisions in front of me and sit down. Reaching into my mind, I feel for that familiar string of magic to grasp.

Suddenly, my eyes fly open. It's not there. For some reason my magic isn't working now. Confused at this place's effects, my face pales and my grasp on the book goes limp. I flip through the pages with renewed urgency, looking for the spell that I found for the barrier. Thankfully, the spell doesn't have to do with my magic, but instead is a verbal and physical spell anyone can do. That means I can only take care of the food after I break the barrier, which means that we have to get out fast or we'll starve to death. I call for Zayne and Quinn and soon they are in the room with me.

"Did you figure it out?" Quinn asks.

"Yeah, there might be a slight problem," I say reluctantly. "I sort of don't have my magic here."

"What? How's that possible?" Zayne asks, alarmed.

"I think it's the barrier. It's acting as a buffer and I can't use my magic while it's there."

"How are we going to get out of here then?" Quinn frowns.

"The good news is that the barrier doesn't need my magic. There are spells that non-mages can create using things around them, and there are also verbal spells. There aren't very many, but, luckily, this is one of them."

"Okay, so what do you need?" Quinn asks calmly, which in turn calms me down. *It will all work out.*

I flip through the book to rediscover the page where I had located the spell. "I packed a lot of these things in my satchel already, so we shouldn't have a problem." Finding the page, I continue, "We need a secret, an object held to heart, and a jar of mist."

"What?" Zayne asks, humored.

I almost roll my eyes. "It's magic. What were you expecting?"

I reach into my satchel and pull out the jar of mist, along with a small pouch.

Muffled whispers emit from the pouch as I carefully

lay it on the floor. Startled, Zayne and Quinn take a step back.

"W- what in the world is that?" Quinn asks.

I look at them like they are stupid. "Secrets."

"Right," Zayne says slowly.

I frown. "The only thing we need now is an object held to heart." I look up from my place on the floor. "Do you guys have anything you keep that holds a lot of significance? That you can't bear losing?" I don't want to use my necklace.

"I might have something." Zayne mutters. He reaches into his shirt and pulls out a necklace of his own. I reach my palm out and he hesitates.

"Worry not," I whisper. "Nothing will happen to it and I will give it back the second I'm done."

With a sigh, he drops the necklace into my palm. The object itself is simple: a leather chord with something that resembles a coin hanging from it. When I look closer, I see the royal emblem of the Kingdom of Elrea. I raise my eyebrow and look up at Zayne, who stiffens when he sees my response. He just whispers, "My mom knew the royal family a long time ago."

I don't push it and instead lay the trinket on the ground, making a triangle with the objects. I close my eyes and mutter some words before stopping and opening the pouch. As I continue murmuring, a wisp escapes the bag and starts gradually expanding until it looks like fog, enveloping the entire room. This wisp is a shade of light blue, which means that it is a happy secret.

I love him, says a feminine voice like glass.

I smile. That's the secret.

Then the fog returns into the form of mist and showers us with a gentle spray of water. Next, I uncap the jar filled with proper mist and pour it onto the ground. All the while, I'm still muttering. The actual mist slowly empties out and covers the floor. Then, in the blink of an eye, the mist turns into a silver liquid. Slowly, it shapes into a wide pentagon with me in the center.

Clutching the necklace in my hand, a pink aura slowly emits from it and I hear someone let out a soft gasp. The pink aura wraps itself on the silver liquid and I quickly take a small dagger from my boot. My skin stings as I quickly slice my hand; I let blood hit the floor. With a mutter, I finish the spell with a few more words, and the liquid and aura disappear as if nothing were there in the first place. I tear some fabric from my clothes and tie it around my hand.

I look up and chuckle under my breath when I see Quinn and Zayne's star-struck expressions. But I'm exhausted. My magic has limits.

"We should check the shield now," I say.

They shake out of their trance and nod in agreement. The star-struck look remains in their eyes as we walk out of the room, into the corridor. The barn is located near the center of the town, so we have to travel for a while to reach the border. Moving quickly, we pack our things, the food and water, and leave the barn. In record time, we are moving through the streets.

They are unusually quiet and I don't spot anyone. I don't think much of it. There is a possibility that the spell made the shadows and "people" disappear as well. Freedom is so close. Soon, we reach the border, but what I see makes me jerk the horse to a stop. Quinn halts on my left, Zayne on my right, and we all gaze at what lies ahead. It's people. Tons of them. Blocking us.

"Can't you blast them or something?" Zayne asks.

I shake my head. "The spell I did back at the barn. It took all my energy."

"Well, what are we going to do?"

I grin. "Can you fight?"

CHAPTER 17
ZAYNE

WREN GRINS AT me. "Can you fight?"

She. Cannot. Be. Serious.

"Well, yes. But that many?" I ask her, looking at the crowd in front of us. They have a look on their faces that screams: *back off.* Their number lines and follows the curve of the border, and stretches on as far as I can see. They're most likely surrounding the entire town.

"Why not?" She grins again and her calm unsettles me. I glance at Quinn but he looks relaxed as usual, like that many people don't bother him.

"And if it's murder you're worried about, it's not that. They're not alive, not really. They're shadows. Once they receive a killing blow, they'll just vanish."

Without another word, she dismounts, and Quinn and I soon follow. I pull out the sword I keep in my sheath, Wren reveals two daggers, and Quinn withdraws his bow and arrows. We approach the crowd. As if something is triggered, they start moving toward us as a single unit in response. The first one approaches me and I swing my sword, hesitating for an instant before stabbing it in the gut. Instantly, the man turns into a shadowy vapor before disappearing completely.

Battle commences. As I finish off another, the same thing happens. Soon, I'm in the zone. Lost in the familiar rhythm. Duck, swing, jab. I repeat it as I ignore the sweat trickling down my face.

Suddenly, at once, there are no more shadow people. In confusion, I break through the haze and look up. All of the shadow people have shifted their positions and are headed in one direction en masse. I catch a glimpse through the crowd and see what – or who - they're headed toward. It's Wren.

She doesn't notice the condensing swarm at first, moving gracefully from one person to the next, barely glancing for more than a second before continuing on. I see one moving from the back, closer than the others, but Wren doesn't appear to notice. I'm about to shout out a warning - but an arrow with green feathers zips through the air and hits them in the back. I glance to the side and see Quinn as he shoots more arrows in quick succession. Snapping out of it, I rush to the crowd around Wren and immerse myself in the fight.

We end up forming a small triangle in the middle with our backs to each other. As a team, we attack. Slowly, the numbers decrease until there is no one left. Relief floods through us as we collapse on the grass. My muscles groan in pain and the reprieve is a blessing. Breathing heavily, I look up at the blue sky.

Once we recover, I realize the town is gone. It's like nothing was ever there in the first place and in its place is a giant clearing. I shudder and jump to my feet. It's time to get out of here.

Once we are far beyond the clearing's bounds, Wren tells us that, with the fight and the spell at the barn, she won't be able to use magic until we find the Lochaere. The Lochaere apparently has enough power to boost her magic again. But we have to eat, so in the end, Wren uses a counter spell on the food. She staggers back and stumbles after doing it, sweat sheening her face. Worried, we ask her if she's okay and she waves it off, sitting down with a grimace. We rest on some logs and eat food, careful to not eat too much even though we are starving.

I'm taking a bite out of the bread when Quinn asks Wren, "So if we run into any more trouble in the next few days, you won't be able to use your magic?"

Wren nods and pauses to swallow her food. "We can't rely on it for *a while*. A while meaning a couple of weeks. I used too much magic in one day and this is the price. But if we get to the Lochaere, it will be able to kick start my magic again and I'll get it back sooner."

I cringe. "So that means we have to keep our eyes open more than before and make sure we stay under the radar."

"It's impossible. We can't hide from him. No one can," Wren says. "I would put a cloaking spell but..." she says, shrugging.

"So, what do you suggest?" I ask her.

She bites her lip as she thinks. Finally, she says, "Well, there's a certain plant that actually can work as a cloaking spell, but it's hard to find. Nonetheless, the plant will cloak you if you have it on your person."

"Well, where can we find it?" I lean forward.

"That's the problem," she says, gulping.

"What? What is it?"

"The plant is in a garden."

"So?" Quinn asks.

She shakes her head. "Not just any garden. It's in the Glasswitch Gardens. It's said to be covered in dark magic and will cause hallucinations in anyone who enters, showing their worst fears. No one who has entered has ever come out."

I let out a low whistle. "You think it's worth it?" I ask her.

"Yes, and I think we can do it. I mean, look at us. We survived the town, didn't we?" she says with a half-smile. "I don't think we have a choice," she adds sadly. "Or else the Sorcerer will definitely find us again. And we won't have a chance against him."

CHAPTER 18
QUINN

THE GLASSWITCH GARDENS are something I've always thought were a myth. People would joke about it at the Compound, saying that if you weren't careful, they'd dump you into the Garden. Dread washes over me, but I stifle it. If we don't do something, we'll be dead anyway.

"Wait a minute," I say as we finish our food. "Where are we exactly?"

Wren blows a stray hair off her face. "I have no idea. I say we start walking though, so the Sorcerer doesn't find us. Our best plan at this point is to walk until we find a road or something."

"How do we know that the Sorcerer won't trick us again and make it look like there is a road?" Zayne asks.

"We don't, but my best guess is that his magic has a limit as well. If he summoned that entire town, it will take a while for him to try something."

"It seems like we don't even have a chance," I say in frustration.

"But, again, when did that ever stop us," Zayne says.

He is right. I never have backed out on anything in my life and I'm not about to start now.

We start walking through the forest, hoping that somehow we'll find a path. One of the first things they taught us at the Compound was that a path always leads to somewhere. What I'm worried about is where this path will take us.

"The detour to the Glasswitch Gardens will delay our journey by a few days, so we must hurry," Wren says as we pick up the pace.

We walk for a few more hours before I hear something. I stop the others with a wave of my hand and gesture for them to be quiet. Again, I hear the sound. Straining my ears, I listen. It is the sound of rushing water. I turn to them excitedly. "There's water nearby." Understanding slowly seeps into their faces.

"Water usually leads to civilization." Zayne says in relief.

We follow the sound of the water until we reach a wide river. We follow the river downstream and talk among ourselves to pass the time. For a while after, there is calm silence, and then Wren jerks to a stop.

I turn to her, confused. "Wren?"

She looks at me with a dazed expression before shaking her head. "I- I thought I saw something."

"What?"

She shakes her head once more as if to clear her thoughts. "Nothing, I'm going crazy."

Just as the words leave her mouth, I see a blur of a shadow at the corner of my vision. In the blink of an eye, a group of shadows block our path. Wren lets out a choking noise and I watch as her face turns green. Suddenly, realization hits me. Her aunt. One shadow steps forward and points a finger at Wren. "Magic welder."

The shadows charge toward us and black swords appear in their hands. The closest one swipes at me and I quickly pull out the sword at my side to block the attack. Our swords clash together before the shadowy male form takes a step back. I go for a swipe at his body, but the sword passes through like there's nothing there.

My body turns cold as he approaches, and I notice from the corner of my eye that Zayne and Wren are doing the same. One of the shadows in front of Wren disappears in a flash before appearing behind her. I barely let out a shout when the shadow lunges for her - but before he can do anything, the necklace around Wren's throat glows brighter than I've ever seen it. Before I know it, a flash of blue light blinds me as it covers the area. When I finally open my eyes, the shadows are gone.

Wren immediately collapses on the floor and any thoughts of the necklace disappear from my mind as Zayne and I rush to her.

"Wren?" Zayne asks gently.

She shakes her head and lets out a shaky breath.

After a couple of minutes, she gets up and silently

begins walking in front of us without saying a word. Zayne and I share a concerned look before following her.

We keep walking until the late evening, and we finally see a town in the distance.

"How do we know this isn't another trap?" I ask.

"Because no matter who this Sorcerer is, they don't have enough power to use additional magic for a while," Wren replies as she quickly puts on a cap and tucks in her hair, so people won't realize that it's a girl wearing men's clothing. Until she finds a place to change, this is our only option. She seems to have gathered herself better while we were trekking. Any sign of distress before was hidden from us, but I can still see that she's hurting inside.

We enter the town and it's similar to the Kingdom of Ulalle. People mill about, tending to their business without sparing a glance at us. Some children laugh as they chase each other, and I smell fresh bread as we pass a bakery. Zayne leads us to the first inn we see that doesn't look run-down. It doesn't look too bad with fresh paint and a friendly atmosphere. We walk in and I smell something like lemon.

As we approach the counter, Zayne asks, "Good morning. Can we get a room?"

The man behind the counter barely gives our dirty clothes a glance as he hands over the keys in exchange for the money the Bennetts had given us. The three of us trek up the stairs and enter a wide hallway with many doors.

Zayne hands us our separate keys and we find the doors that correspond with the number engraved on them. Zayne turns out to be in the room across the hallway from me, and Wren in the room to my left. We decide that the best course of action is to first take a much-needed bath, and we enter our separate rooms. As close the door behind me, I smile to see clean sheets and a bed. Oh, the small things taken for granted.

There is an adjoining room and I see that there is a bath already drawn. I test the water with my finger and find that it's cold. Not that I mind. A chilly bath just might be what I need right now. I take off my clothes and relax into the cool water with a sigh.

CHAPTER 19

WREN

THE MEMORY OF the shadows still haunts me as I remember my aunt. However, I push it to the back of my mind as I pull out the small black book of maps from my satchel, having already taken a bath. Being clean is a privilege and it feels good to be fresh again.

I flip through the thin pages that crinkle. I need to discern the location of this town, so I can see exactly how far we are from the Glasswitch Gardens. When we walked in, I noted a sign, which showed that we are in the town of Onryx.

Finally, I discover a map that includes this town. I remember Aunt Adnis telling me that they are near the Vryhs Mountains. I hold my breath in anticipation, but then my stomach drops. It is a ten-day hike. We don't have enough time for that. I think hard about another option. We have to find the Glasswitch Gardens or we have to call it off.

I'm about to get up when I freeze. A memory flashes

before my eyes as I remember my mother sitting beside my bed, telling me stories of places and different creatures. One of them was about the Glasswitch Gardens.

"How do you find the Glasswitch Gardens, Mama?"

"That's the thing. You don't, Wren." She smiles slightly. "The Glasswitch Gardens find you. If you have the whole heart to go there, then it will find you. All you have to do is walk. But no one wants to go there and they shouldn't. They don't ever come back. But I guess 'have to' and 'want to' are completely different things, aren't they?" she says with a sad smile.

A chill runs through me as the memory fades. We have to go. And I think there is truth in what she said. All we have to do is get on the road and then keep on trekking with the full want and desire to reach the Glasswitch Gardens – all without fear overcoming us. We will die if we let our fears control us, and that's what I'm worried about. I hurry downstairs to where we each agreed to meet after bathing. I walk into the common area and immediately spot the others at a table in the corner. I slide in the booth as a waiter approaches us.

"What would you all like?" she asks.

"Some bread and cheese and meat would be nice, thank you," Zayne tells her. She nods and hurries away.

"So, where are we?" Quinn asks me.

"We're in the town of Onryx."

I watch as Quinn's eyebrows rise in surprise. "We're way off the course."

I sigh. "I know." I continue and tell them how I think we can find the Gardens.

Zayne's eyebrows bunch together and he asks. "Are you sure this is going to work?"

I sigh. "Do you really think we have a choice? Plus, most of what my parents told me always held special meaning. I don't think my mom just told me that as a bedtime story."

"Never mind how we get there," Quinn interjects. "What are we going to do about the fear part? You are not the only person who has heard stories of the Gardens. They say that whoever goes in will go mad, because they are faced with fears they didn't even know they had." A grim look passes over his eyes. "They die from madness, Wren."

I sigh and blow a stray piece of hair from my face. "I know. You guys don't have to come with me."

Quinn shakes his head. "If you go, I go. I don't have choice."

Confused, I ask, "What do you mean?"

Quinn pauses and then replies, "The Sorcerer killed my parents. I'm going. I'm just worried. We won't do any good if we're dead."

Zayne interjects, "So, the idea is that we just, what? Start walking and we'll magically appear there?"

"Yes, the Gardens are portrayed as one living thing that the witches from the Glasswitch clan made a long time ago."

"Wait, witches are real?" Quinn asks in shock. Zayne shakes his head in disbelief.

"Well, yes," I say slowly.

"How are they different from enchanters?" Zayne asks curiously.

"A witch's magic isn't a part of them. They use what you guys describe as black magic. And they're not friendly. At all. When you see a witch, you're almost as good as dead. I've never seen one, but they are said to have teeth as sharp as knives and are some of the cleverest things alive."

Zayne laughs uneasily. "Hopefully we don't meet one."

"What type of things did your parents tell you as a child?" Quinn asks in alarm.

I just shrug, but I can't shake the sensation of fear at what is awaiting us in the Gardens.

"We have to start as soon as possible," I say, ignoring the feeling that something is going to go wrong.

Quinn shakes his head. "First we rest."

That's the best idea I've ever heard.

I wake up to the sound of fast breathing and open my eyes to look at the blank ceiling. I glance to my right and a scream gets stuck in my throat when I see a shadow. I quickly sit up. "Who is it?"

The shadow steps up to the light and I relax when I see that it's Quinn. His hands are behind his back and he just looks at me. I stare back at him in confusion.

"Why are you in my room?"

"I just came to check in on you, but saw that you were sleeping. I was just about to leave when you woke up."

"Oh, okay," I say, still confused. I squint at him. "Was there anything you wanted to tell me?"

Quinn shifts uncomfortably. "It can wait," he says finally and leaves the room.

CHAPTER 20
ZAYNE

IT SCARES AND amazes me how many things are out there that we don't even know exist. Things that can kill us in the blink of an eye. The blunt honesty of everything is that I am afraid. We headed up into our rooms after we ate, and the second I reach my room, sleep takes its hold on me.

This inn is amazing; it even has a few books on the table for a guest. I look at them longingly, knowing that I won't be able to sit and just read for a while. I turn toward the bed when I hear a thud. I turn around, alarmed to see that one of the books has fallen to the floor.

Crazy that I was just thinking- no. The wind must have blown it over. I glance at the window and see that it's open. I am just getting paranoid with everything that is going on. I sigh and return the book to the table. I walk to the bed and sink into the mattress. Relief floods through me, but as I go to sleep, I can't shake off this weird feeling.

The next morning, we all meet up at the same table as before. Wren is the only one there when I arrive. Sliding in, I ask her, "Where's Quinn?"

"He said he had something to do and he'll be back soon."

Slight suspicion enters my thoughts, but I push it away. I am really on edge lately. "Do you know what for?" I ask her.

"No, I didn't ask. It's not my business I guess." She shrugs.

I frown, but say nothing.

"So, do you have family?" she asks.

I tense and glance at her. "Yes. Both my parents and my brother and sister."

She smiles sadly. "I wish I had that. What are your siblings like?"

I smile and tell her, "My sister. She's a wild one. Always looking to break the rules. And she always makes everyone around her laugh. My brother is the one everyone can't help but love and he's one of the smartest people I know. He always has an answer and I know I can trust him. He's the most responsible one. Always telling us to be careful. He's older than me and my sister's the youngest one." My smile disappears. "I haven't seen them in a while. Because of the Gavreel Society."

"So how did the Gavreel Society start anyway?" she asks.

"Well I guess you can say the royal family kind of hired me to make a group to find the cause of the deaths," I say slowly.

"Oh really?"

"Yeah, as you know, I'm from the Kingdom of Elrea. I'm one of the soldiers there."

Her eyes grow wide. "But that's where we're headed. Where the–"

"Lochaere is? Yeah, I know," I say, rubbing a hand across my face.

"But that means you can meet your family again, right?"

"Yeah," I say, smiling slightly. That's what I'm worried about.

"Hey, guys," a deep voice says above us. We look up to see Quinn.

"Where did you go?" I ask him, curious.

"I just needed some fresh air," he says quickly and slides in next to Wren. He is hiding something, but I decide not to push it.

"So, what's the plan?" Wren asks us.

"I think we should gather our stuff, eat something, and head on our way. The sooner we leave, the sooner we get there," Quinn offers up.

"We aren't catching a break," Wren says, sighing. "But there will be a day when this is all over and it will be worth it." It sounds like she is assuring herself more than us.

"Well, we should probably stop by the market as well, to buy more food and to restock supplies," I say.

Wren nods. "I need to go to some herb shops and places as well, just in case we need them for spells."

"Well, we can go there now," Quinn suggests.

We all agree and after ordering and eating some food, we get up after leaving a few coins on the table. We walk through the dirty streets, Quinn on one side of Wren and myself on the other. Making quick time, we are soon in the square.

The square has many stalls and people shouting out about their wares, urging passersby that they should buy something or else regret it. We walk around until we finally discover a shop named, 'A Thistle of Herbs.' The place itself is scary. The windows are tinted black and the words are golden. The locale as a whole is the highest level of creepy. One of the windows even has something that appears to be eyes, but I hope that's not what it is. I shudder and we step in.

A small bell chimes as the wooden door creaks slowly open. Cool, dusty air rushes at us, but otherwise, there are no signs of life. The only source of light down here is a small, dingy candle on the counter. Silence greets us.

"Hello? Is anyone there?" Quinn yells.

"Maybe we should leave," I whisper.

Wren nods uneasily, but before we can exit, we hear a deep male voice call out, "No, please feel free to stay."

We turn to the voice and see a form within the shadows. It steps forward and reveals itself as a young man with brown hair, walking into the only circle of light. He is what most people would call 'blessed with good looks.' His clothes show that, despite the appearance of the shop, he is actually quite rich. He gives a wolfish grin and there's a slight pause in the air.

Wren hesitantly thanks him and turns to the shelves

filled with herbs. Quinn and I continue to stare at him as he stares at us. When he provides a calm smile, I roll my eyes. We continue this odd staring contest until Wren finishes selecting the herbs she needs and walks to the counter. Quinn and I move warily toward the counter as well, putting our hands on the hilt of our swords in caution, and the man takes notices, chuckling under his breath as his blue eyes twinkle in amusement. Wren places the jars on the counter with a thud.

"A long journey, I presume?" the man asks while he counts the coins.

We all exchange a look, and then Wren pulls her eyes away and cautiously says, "I guess you can say that."

"I can tell from your clothes." He turns to Wren then and says, "You look familiar."

Startled, Wren tries to hide her surprise and fails. "I get that a lot," she answers finally. "But I was just about to say the same to you. You look like someone I used to know."

I raise my eyebrows at the exchange and glace at Quinn to see my surprise reflected on his face as well.

"Where are you from?" he asks.

Wren's eyes squint with suspicion. Maybe she isn't stupid after all. "Where are you from?"

He laughs. "All right, I understand. But you remind me of a girl I used to know in the village where I lived. We used to be best friends..." He laughs uneasily and runs his hand through his hair. "Never mind, this is crazy. It's just that she was the most important person in my life. Her name was Wr-"

Wren cuts him off with a shake of her head and she backs up, continuing the motion. I see her bottom lip shake before she asks in a small voice, "Thomas?"

His eyes soften and a huge grin appears on his face. "I was wondering when you would catch up."

Something is off about him, but I can't put my finger on it.

A sob escapes Wren's mouth and she reaches across the counter to hug him tightly. After whispering a few hushed words, Wren asks him, "I thought you were dead."

Thomas laughs dryly. "Not quite."

If I wasn't watching him so closely, I would have missed the quick glance he shot Quinn's way. Quinn notices too and stiffens slightly.

I stash that bit of information in my brain for later, but I soon forget as Wren starts talking again.

"Thomas, this is Zayne and this is Quinn."

"It's nice to meet you, gentleman," Thomas says kindly.

We don't respond but Wren gives him a wide smile.

CHAPTER 21
QUINN

WHAT IS HE doing here? What are the odds that he knew Wren? Does he know about the Enchanters' Child and that she is the very one he has his arm around now? A surge of something way too close to jealousy sneaks in at that, but I ignore it. The questions turn in a never-ending circle. Why is he here?

'Thomas' looks back at Zayne and I as we walk back to the inn. His eyes latch on to mine for a brief second and I immediately make my face into a blank slate. It doesn't slip my attention that Zayne notices the exchange. Thomas is ruining everything.

We finally catch up to them as we near the inn and I hear Thomas ask Wren, "So what are you doing here anyway? This is a long way from the village, isn't it?"

"I was headed to a market in another kingdom that's pretty popular right now. I happened to meet these kind gentlemen on my way there," Wren says smoothly.

I feel a hint of pride but that is followed with confusion. I am worried about the well-being of someone I'm supposed to kidnap. I am just as bad as Thomas, maybe even worse. I had entered Wren's room last night with a knife in my hand, intending to finish the job just to get it over with. It was the perfect opportunity because she didn't have magic and Zayne was in his room. I could have forced her to follow me out of the inn and back to the Compound. But then she woke up and I couldn't do it with her watching me. I hid the knife behind my back. For some reason, the idea of taking Wren in her sleep is more appealing than doing it while she looks at me with betrayal. That thought leaves me with remorse.

I can't risk having emotions like this. So much is at risk and I love my sister more than anything. I would do anything for her safety. But I can't help wonder if there's no other way.

As we enter the inn, Wren and Zayne excuse themselves to pack up for the trip.

Wren looks back when she reaches the stairs. "Are you coming?"

I smile at her. "I'll be there in a second."

She frowns for a moment, but nods and walks up the stairs. As soon as she does, I face Thomas and ask him with concealed anger, "What are you doing here?" At least he doesn't know I'm the Black Assassin.

"Relax," he says, but I just tense up more. "Damien sent me to find you and deliver a message. He just asked me to say: 'Have you found it yet?' Whatever that means." He narrows his eyes at me. "I know I'm just a messenger and not supposed to ask questions about whatever you assassins do, but - what are you doing with the likes of them? Wren's a good person."

My lips tighten into a thin line. After a pause, I ask the question that keeps nagging me. "Surprising that you met your friend while searching for me." It isn't a surprise that he did find me. That shop is assassin-owned. Damien has a messenger stationed at various shops and he must have asked all of them to relay the message if they saw me. I usually don't know the messengers personally, but Thomas here is an exception.

"I don't know what you're up to, but don't you dare hurt Wren. Just finish your business and leave her alone," he says with vehemence.

I smile sadly on the inside. Little does he know that she is the business that I need to take care of. If I had a choice, I wouldn't hurt her or any of the other people Damien has blackmailed me into killing. But that doesn't make it right. I hate him and I hate myself.

Without saying a word, I turn from Thomas and walk away, up the stairs and back to my room. One thought follows me: I want a better life, but does someone like me deserve it? As I enter the corridor upstairs I see Wren about to enter her room and she gives me a curious glance. I give her a reassuring smile and she gives a gentle smile in return.

"Remember," she whispers to us, "walk with whole heart."

I take a deep breath. I have faced thousands and conquered all. I taught myself throughout my entire life that fear has no place in my heart. Fear is weakness – but right now, it seems like all of that has burned to ash. For the first time, since that night when I was a little, I'm afraid.

We start walking and don't talk as we leave the town and, with it, safety. Wren reaches for Zayne's hand on her left and mine on her right, and we continue walking like that down the road. I squeeze her hand and think about finding the plant, about how – without it – we will be dead. And I won't be any good to anyone dead. I frown for a second. Or maybe I am better off dead. I shake my head from the cold truth and think about the garden. How it will help Wren and how maybe I can do something good in my life. I like to think so.

Suddenly, I feel a chill and the world goes black. Surprisingly, all I feel is numbness. It's too late to turn back now. The only comfort is the warmth of Wren's hand in mine. As fast as it had come, the darkness vanishes. I look around, startled, and realize that this must be the Gardens. Yet a garden is far from what this is. Dead flowers cluster the area and the air itself has a dusty smell. I shiver at the sudden change in temperature. Black fences surround us and there is a thick fog.

I turn to Zayne and Wren to see how they're reacting to it, but alarm shoots through me when I realize they're gone. I swallow hard. I look down and take a panicked step back as I see black smoke rise up from the ground. But fear doesn't have time to wash over me as I pass out.

CHAPTER 22

WREN

I SLOWLY OPEN MY eyes from my position on the ground in confusion. I blink rapidly as my vision returns into focus. I jerk up with a start when I realize I'm at the cottage. Why am I on the floor? The sensation that I'm forgetting something is strong, but that disappears just as fast as it had come when I hear footsteps on the dirt floor.

I quickly get up and brush the dirt off my trousers. Straining to hear the noise, I follow the sound to find its origin. I notice a sliver of a skirt turning the corner, and a sensation of longing hits me. I hurry to catch up to her, my bare feet snuffing out any noise. I look around the corner warily and see a door at the end of a hallway. A woman is walking toward it and, startled, I realize it's my mother.

She quietly opens the door and I see my father on the other side. Somehow, I feel a tense sensation in the air and stay where I am. Somewhere in my mind, this seems familiar, but that's crazy. She whispers something to him and they reach toward a black box I hadn't seen before.

Darkness appears to seep out of it and I shiver with terror. I freeze and watch the box, transfixed. The box begins to shake before breaking. A shriek emits from the dark entity that rises from the container. In a blink, the entity is gone and is replaced with a shadow. The shadow reaches out a hand, red emitting from its chest, and I watch with alarm as blue wisps escape from my parents' mouths and they collapse to the ground. As I stumble down the hallway, blood slowly begins seeping out of the box and I blink, horrified.

Abruptly, there's a blast, and the force shoves me into the wall. I groan with pain from my position, and with bleary eyes, I look at the box. It had opened and the dark shadow is in front of it. The shadow gradually shifts and, before my eyes, turns into the shape of a human. I scramble to my feet and am about to run when the hallway starts tilting. I wince in pain as my body hits the floor and then the wall, over and over again.

Suddenly, the world goes gray and the cottage disappears. The only thing apart from the gray is the shadow in front of me. The same darkness and power emits from it, so overwhelmingly strong that it weighs me down. The shadow begins moving toward me and I try to step back when I realize with panic that I can't move.

They were weak, your parents. I enjoyed destroying them, a voice in my mind says. My eyes widen as I realize that it's the shadow talking to me. *How foolish they were, to think that they could defeat me. And now the entire world is depending on their little daughter. A weakling who can't do anything,* the voice says in contempt.

I shake my head in denial. "Stop!" I scream. "Stop it!"

Worthless and useless and incapable. You're going to be the one responsible for the destruction of the world because YOU are too weak.

I squeeze my eyes shut tightly and grit my teeth together. I feel blood in my mouth and realize I'm biting the inside of my cheek.

I shake my head again. "No. No. You're the one responsible, not m- me. You." A tear slides down my cheek.

How disappointed your parents must be if they saw you now?

The shadow reaches out with a black hand and grips my neck, raising me off the floor. I start choking and soon I see dark circles in my vision.

Then I remember. This isn't real. This isn't real. I force myself to stay calm and remember that I have magic. Maybe, even though it's not working in the real world, it works here in this one. I reach inside myself, feeling for what I've always thought of as my source of magic. I mutter the one spell of light I know. Hopefully, because it's darkness, it'll work.

Light shines through my hands and the shadow releases me.

I fall to the ground with a thud and the room fades away instead to reveal a dreary garden that I had seen before the black smoke arrived. I look around for Quinn and Zayne, but they aren't here. Where are they? Worry hits me, but all I can do is wait.

CHAPTER 23
ZAYNE

I FEEL SOMETHING COOL on my cheek and, in confusion, I push off the ground. I look down and it is a marble floor. I look around, perplexed. I'm at home. Weird that I'm on the floor though. I walk up the intricate stairs in front of me and see one of the family's maids at the top. Her name is Mary and we've talked a few times. My sister and she are best friends.

She makes eye contact with me before walking down the corridor. There is something off about the house. It's eerily quiet, so much so that a pin drop would be violently loud. A sudden feeling of unease floods through me, but it immediately disappears. Looking around, I wonder where everyone is. Usually there are many people walking around the place. My father is a powerful man with many connections.

Confused, I walk through the same corridor my maid had gone down, because that is the way to my room and if I see her again I can ask her where everyone is. I walk down the corridor and the plush carpet mutes my steps. I finally arrive in front of my door and I see that it is slightly open. I frown. The only person to ever go in there is me unless I give someone permission. Even the maids don't enter. Too many secrets they aren't supposed to know.

I cautiously nudge the door and it creaks open. I step in cautiously and look around the room. Everything is in place, and I start to think that I was paranoid. I walk to a set of glass doors and into my sitting room. Suddenly, I feel weightless before I crash into the floor. Confused, I put my hand on the ground to push myself up, but then I feel something sticky. Hesitantly, I lift my hand to my face and, in horror, see red that looks suspiciously like blood.

I whip my head to see where it comes from, and I glimpse Mary face-down on the floor. Fear spikes through me, and I run to her, to see if she's okay. I approach and hold my breath as I reach out to touch her. The second my hand touches her shoulder, she shudders.

"Mary?" I ask gently.

Suddenly, she swivels around and lets out a blood-curling scream. The veins in her neck pop out, and her eyes are bloodshot. Blood comes in tears out of her eyes as her nails claw at the floor. I step back when I see the gaping wound now running from her ear to her chin. It looks like someone took a knife and slashed her face. I gulp slowly, and my eyes dart down to her now-exposed shoulder and see another wound. Mutely, I realize that someone had carved a triangle and arrow into her shoulder. The same triangle and arrow that I see on the bodies I have been tracking with the Gavreel Society.

I hear a pounding on the door, but I don't risk turning my back on her. I keep my eyes on Mary as I slowly retreat away. But for every step I take backward, she takes one forward. I hear a loud thud and a crash, and finally I risk a glance back. Through the glass doors, I see shadows and pay more attention, but then I hear a crash from behind. I whip my head back to look at Mary and see a shattered vase now at her feet. I hear the glass door creak open and see a blur rush into the room.

I blink and suddenly many people have joined Mary. They all stare at me, and in alarm I realize that they all are in the same state as Mary. As I look closer at their faces, I freeze. I recognize a lot of them from the files that I've collected on the dead. I look at Aldwin Thomas, the first one I had found in the woods near Stealburrow. He was-*is* a noble.

How are they alive? There's no way. Mary should be dead as well. Aldwin makes a low noise in his throat and all of them perk up. Well, that can't be good. There's a slight pause in the air where it feels like time itself stands still. Then it breaks as all of them run toward me. I snap out of the shock and run to the sword that is leaning against the wall next to my bed. I grasp it just as I feel a hand on my ankle.

In panic, I shake my leg and the grip loosens. I take my sword and immediately go into the familiar pattern, but instead of killing them, I just hurt them so they don't reach me. I glance at the door that leads to the hallway.

I have to get out of here. Slowly I make my way around the room, all the while they attack me. Surprisingly, they aren't that hard to ward off. Their robotic movements don't give them the advantage.

I finally am close enough to the door, and I dive over the threshold before getting up quickly and shutting the door with a slam. I pull on the handles with force so they don't get out and quickly slide my blade through to use as a deadbolt. I step back and, in relief, see that it worked.

Before another thought goes through my mind, my home fades away and I quickly realize that I'm back in the Glasswitch Gardens. I wipe the sweat off my forehead, look around, and I sigh in relief when I see Wren pacing worriedly. I clear my throat, and her head whips up. A look of relief washes over her face when she sees me.

"You made it," she says, smiling.

I just nod in shock, and she shakes her head miserably.

"I know," she declares simply.

I join her as she continues to pace again. Now we wait for Quinn.

CHAPTER 24

QUINN

I FEEL GROGGY AS I slowly blink my way into consciousness. I wince because my head aches. My face lies on something soft and moist, and I become aware of the sound of crickets as well as the dry summer air. I sit up and look around in confusion. The dark sky twinkles with thousands of stars that shine like diamonds. Stubs of vegetation and large stalks surround me, while a poorly built wire fence encloses the property.

Why am I sleeping outside on our farm? I roll my neck to try and get rid of the crick in it, but this doesn't work. I twist to the left and see our cottage in the distance, a warm source of light shining through the windows. I get up and brush the dirt off my breeches. I wiggle my toes through the dirt and enjoy the small massage on my bare feet. I run a hand through my mud-caked hair. I should head back. Ma and Papa might be wondering where I went.

I head down the path and softly whistle under my

breath. A fleeting thought that something isn't right passes through my mind, but I dismiss it. It's probably because I just spent most of the night sleeping outside. As I near the house, I hear a loud crash and I jump. I pause in fear before I run toward the cottage. Papa and Ma. I approach the house and barely have time to register that the door is off its hinges before I rush in. The main room is empty and eerie. I hear another thud in their bedroom and I rush toward it.

I burst in and, immediately, my eyes land on the ginormous thing in the center of the room. Yes, 'thing.' Because I don't have the words to exactly describe what it is. Terror seizes my heart as I take in the black entity with sharp yellow teeth. Its ruby eyes turn to look at me as it slowly realizes there is someone else in the room. Its sharp, pointy ears perk up and it takes one step toward me. Its razor-like claw sinks into the dirt floor and I see a glimpse of a tail that has what looks like thousands of daggers jutting out of its skin.

I hear a small cry in the corner of the room, and I turn my head. I let out a sob as I see Ma slumped on the floor, leaning against the wall. Blood streams down her face and out of her nose. "Quinn?" she asks in shock as her blue eyes widen. Slowly, horror washes over her face and she screams, "Run!"

But I'm frozen and my eyes again lock with the creature. Yet, once more, something distracts me. Absently, I realize that Ma's cries slowly start to fade away. Behind the beast is something that looks like a lump. The longer I stare, the more I realize with numb shock that it's Papa. A gaping hole is in the center of his chest, his face petrified in an eternal scream. Anger stabs through me and I look at the beast.

It takes one step toward me and sniffs as I step back. Anger, however, is immediately replaced by fear as the beast lunges toward me. I roll out of the way just in time and the beast quickly pivots in my direction. I look around in panic and my eyes land on the wooden chest across the room. Papa always keeps his sword in there. He used to be some sort of soldier for the king. Sometimes we would go outside and he would teach me things.

Tears fill my eyes, but I quickly blink them away. I hear a growl and I'm again thrown into the present. The beast approaches me and I sprint across the room, praying that this isn't the end for me. I slide onto my knees and ignore the sting it brings. With trembling hands, I wrench the chest open. It creaks as the lid thuds against the wall.

The sword lies peacefully on top of cloth, and the steel glints in the light. I quickly grasp it and turn back toward the beast just in time to see it lunge at me again. I leap to the side, making sure that I don't turn my back on it. It lets out a deep growl, and saliva drips from its mouth. I grit my teeth and narrow my eyes. What am I doing? I'm an assassin. The Black Assassin, and I've got to get a grip. The Black Assassin would've already killed the beast. I let out a yell and lunge at the creature. It dives at me at the same time, but instead of attacking, I slide between its legs and come up behind it.

Before it can react, I leap onto its back and cling on as

the beast growls and shakes around, trying to make me let go. I bang my head on the side of the beast and I let out a soft groan. I feel the sword begin to slip, and I tighten my hold. Lifting the sword, I plunge it into the beast. I wait for something to happen, but the beast continues to swing as if nothing has changed. I frown and look around for its weak spot. I see a light in the corner of my eyes and turn to the source.

For the first time, I notice a faint purple sign on the back of the monster's neck. Maybe that's the weak spot. Abandoning the sword, I reach into my boot and feel the handle of my dagger. I grasp onto it and pull it free. I crawl up the creature's back and am suddenly jerked forward as it takes a large step. I tighten my hold and close my eyes. Once it tires, again I continue moving.

Finally, I reach the glowing sign and tighten my grip on the dagger. I plunge it deep into the center. For a second, nothing happens and my heart sinks. But then the beast shrieks eerily like a human, and just like that, it turns to black ash. I start falling, but before I can hit the floor, the room disappears and the ground is replaced with the dirt of the Glasswitch Gardens. I crash into steady earth and groan in pain. I roll onto my back and take a few deep breaths.

"Quinn?" I hear a relieved voice ask. I don't respond, but then Wren and Zayne appear and their anxious expressions fill my vision.

"Oh, you're alive!" Wren exclaims in relief.

"Can't get rid of me that easily," I say with a crooked grin.

"Glad you're okay, good friend," Zayne says with a grin of his own.

I cringe on the inside. I don't deserve their happiness at seeing me alive. My mind turns back to what had happened. That creature was the one that killed my parents. It was like that night all over again. I shudder and push it to the back of my mind. I get up and look at Wren. "So where is the plant we went through all of that for?"

"I was just talking with Zayne about this before you showed up. I think we have to walk again with the wholehearted desire. But now it's for the plant, not the Gardens."

I'm about to nod, but then I pause. "Wait, you *think*?" Unbelievable.

"Why couldn't we have just done the desire thing with the plant in the first place? Why go through the Gardens?" Zayne inquires.

Wren shakes her head. "It's hard to explain, but if we tried to do that, we would've felt something like an invisible barrier preventing us from going straight to the flower. I think it is a way for the witches to make sure that it's protected." She bites her lip in nervousness. "Just believe me. I think this will work."

"It better," I mutter under my breath.

Wren raises her eyebrows and asks, "What was that?"

"Oh nothing," I say with an innocent smile.

She rolls her eyes and gestures for each of us to take her hand again. We are all in the same position as when we got here, and again, we start walking into the unknown.

CHAPTER 25
WREN

OH PLEASE, PLEASE work. I repeat in my head. The daggers Quinn is shooting at my head aren't helping. None of us talk about what we had seen or what happened in the dreams. I think it's for the best. As we walk, the temperature seems to drop with every step. Soon, we start to shiver and there seems to be no end to the garden.

"This is stupid," Zayne grits out.

"I second that," Quinn adds.

I'm about to call it off when suddenly I feel a gush of warm wind, and then, in a blink of an eye, we are in a lush garden with many flowers. It's something out of a dream. Quinn lets out a low whistle, and we look around in amazement. The drastic contrast to the Gardens we were originally in to this one is astonishing. A sweet honey smell envelops the air, and many butterflies flutter around.

"Where are we?" I ask in amazement.

Zayne looks around. "How do we know which one is the plant we need?"

"We should probably walk around and see if we can find it." I say, eager to explore.

Zayne nods. "Okay."

We walk around the garden, aweing at everything. The most beautiful flowers surround us, varying from roses of different colors to Amaryllis. I grin at the variety of plants. Aunt Adnis would have jumped with joy if she saw this place and the number of different herbs here just at our fingertips. If we had a place like this, we could say goodbye to all those heartless nights and burning days of scraping for enough herbs to earn a living.

We enter a green clearing and in the middle is a small folly. Zayne slowly wanders off to the corner of the clearing to further explore, leaving me with Quinn.

"Someone lives here, or used to," I say, gesturing to the folly.

"True, we should probably get what we need and go," he says, but he doesn't make a move at all. "Want to take a walk?" he asks.

Even though we know we should probably leave, I think that some part of us needs the reprieve. I shrug. "Sure."

We head down a path and continue walking in comfortable silence. Quinn is the first one to break the quiet. "How are the daggers?"

I shake my head. "I never got to thank you."

"No, it's my pleasure," he says with a small smile.

I am about to ask him what he meant – when he said he did bad things in the past – but I decide against it. I wouldn't want people asking me about my past either. Instead, I ask, "So how did you learn to use a bow and arrow? You're really skilled at it."

A shadow passes over Quinn's face, and I feel regret. "I could ask you the same thing," he replies.

"I'm sorry. I shouldn't have asked," I quickly say, knowing that it's a delicate subject for him by the painful look on his face.

"No, you didn't do anything wrong," he says, shaking his head. "My father was a soldier. He was really good with the sword and was good at the bow and arrow as well."

I don't say anything. I know what it feels like to lose someone. Even though I want to, I don't ask what happened to his parents. He smiles sadly at me and reveals, "He was in my hallucination."

I pause and then let out a sigh. "Yeah, so were my parents. I guess we aren't that different, are we?"

"No, we are. Trust me," he says with grim seriousness. There's a huge secret he's keeping. I can see it in his eyes, but I keep my questions contained for once. Something bad happened to him, and my heart aches at the thought.

We continue to walk around for another few minutes when we hear Zayne shout to us.

"Guys?" he yells.

"Coming!" I scream back.

Finally, we find Zayne back at the clearing.

"What is it?" Quinn asks.

"Was that there before?" Zayne asks with worry as he points toward the folly.

We follow his hand and, at first, I don't understand.

"I don't see anything," I confess warily.

"No, not the folly." He shakes his head. "The flower that's before it."

I shift my gaze to the ground and see what he's talking about. The flower itself seems to glow and has an orange hue to it. The petals are beautiful and tilted outwards. Recognition hits me.

"That's it. That's the flower," I say in excitement. I start to head toward it, but Zayne grasps my arm.

"Wren, wait. It can't be that easy."

"Easy? We went through life-threating hallucinations just to get here."

"Still…" Worry fills his eyes.

"It'll be fine," I say, and he finally releases his hold on me.

I run to the flower and quickly pluck it out of the ground. The plant rests in my hand as I show it to them. "See? No problem." I shove the flower into my satchel, but the second I do that, I feel a strong gust of wind.

"Oh, not again," Zayne says.

Cold air hits me again, and suddenly we are back in the original Glasswitch Gardens.

"Okay, we have what we need. Let's go." I step forward, but when they don't make a move to follow me, I give them a confused look. "What?"

"Uh, Wren?" Quinn says slowly.

He points beyond my shoulder. I whip around and

find myself face to face with a witch. White hair surrounds her in a halo and the rest of her body is like a shadow as she hovers above the ground. Fear shoots through me.

You're not getting away that easily, Child of Magic. The voice echoes in my mind, and I take a step back toward Zayne and Quinn.

"What are we going to do?" I ask in panic.

"The only thing we can do. Fight," Quinn replies, but I can hear the worry in his voice.

The witch raises her hand, revealing nails like daggers, and approaches us. As she opens her mouth, I see a glimpse of razor-sharp teeth that match her nails. I gulp. We're doomed.

Then the witch shimmers and disappears. Gasping, I look around in alarm. For a moment, the world is still and silent. I am hoping for too much if I, for a second, think she's gone. Because she isn't. Witches never leave a fight. I've never heard of someone that was successful when it comes to killing a witch. I shove the horrible thought of the unlikeliness that we're going to survive into the back of my mind. We've come this far. We can't die now. I take out my dagger when, suddenly, I hear the sound of silver against silver and turn around.

The witch's face greets me. I hold back a scream and duck as she swings her hand in my direction.

You may have passed the hallucinations, but that isn't the scariest part. I am, the same voice from earlier says.

Taking clues from the gasps emitting from Quinn and Zayne, I deduce that, this time, they hear the voice as well.

"Oh, we are so dead," I mutter.

"Not helping, Wren," Zayne reminds me.

I roll my shoulders to relieve some tension, but it doesn't work. Fear rattles through me to a point that I begin shaking. I flashback to all those stories Aunt Adnis told me. Like that one about the witch who burned down an entire village because someone made the mistake of jeering at her. They're also incapable of love and forgiveness. The only thing they know is anger and death. I was hoping that I would never have to face one of these, but here I am, about to fight one. And how are the others so calm right now?

CHAPTER 26

ZAYNE

I'M FREAKING OUT. At least if I die, my father will finally notice me. I chuckle at the grim thought and, out of the corner of my eye, I see Quinn glance at me like I'm crazy. I ignore him. And Rose, she would be devastated. No. We're going to get through this. We. Are. Not. Going. To. Die. I repeat the sentence over and over again when, suddenly, the witch disappears.

The blood leaves my face. I stifle the noise making its way up my throat. I still have my pride and don't plan to lose it, but that plan is starting to turn to dust. Days ago, I didn't even know witches existed and now I'm facing one? It's amazing the amount of life-threatening incidents we've been in. And ridiculous.

"Has anyone ever survived a witch attack?" I ask, hoping to be comforted.

Wren pauses. "Sure," she drags out.

So that's a no. Well, that didn't help. The witch appears

once more in front of Wren, and she swings her dagger but misses as the witch ducks to the side. The witch's mouth turns into what I think is a smirk. This is a game to her. She disappears once more and we slowly move closer to each other until we form a triangle with our backs to each other. We cautiously move in a circle, looking for the witch. Waiting.

All of a sudden, the witch is in front of me and swipes before I can register anything. She aims at my face and I duck, but not before she grazes my cheek. I wince at the sting it produces and bring my hand up to my face. I gulp when I see the blood coating my fingers.

"Zayne?" Wren asks in concern.

"I'm okay," I hope.

The witch pauses. What's she waiting for? She could have killed us in seconds. There's another sudden temperature drop and a brush of cold winds. I hope that doesn't mean what I think it means.

Something moves in the corner of my eye, but when I turn my head to look, there is nothing there. I swing my head back and shout at Quinn and Wren in fear. Standing next to the witch are five more just like her. There is no way we can get out of this. Wren and Quinn break the triangle and stand at either side of me. We all take a step back when the witches begin floating closer.

"I failed my parents," Wren says so quietly that I almost don't hear her.

I say nothing. I failed too.

The witches grow so close that I can see the hunger in

their eyes. The witch who was here first leads them, and she looks at Wren.

I've always wondered how your kind tastes, she says into our minds, and Wren's face turns white. Just as the witch raises her hand to turn Wren into ribbons, I almost succumb to the fact that we are going to die. But suddenly I see a flash of blue. I blink my eyes, but the blue light is still there.

What? I look around and jolt when I realize that Wren's necklace is glowing again. This knowledge slowly dawns on Wren as well and her eyes widen. We all stand transfixed on the stone around her neck. Even the witch pauses when she notes the blue light and, suddenly, she lets out a high screech before turning to dust.

Relief hits me, and I almost sink to my knees. Quickly, however, confusion replaces it. Quinn and I turn to Wren in shock. "How? What?" I ask.

"Don't look at me. I have no idea," Wren says.

"Well, obviously that isn't just an ordinary necklace," I say and I remember how it had done the same thing with the people of shadow.

She rubs her neck. "Well, it isn't."

Quinn narrows his eyes at her. "And what exactly is it, then?"

"The other half of the Lochaere," she mumbles softly and I almost don't catch what she says.

Quinn and I look at each other. "You mean to tell us that you've had half of it the entire time?" Quinn asks.

"I didn't think it was important."

Quinn shakes his head in frustration. "Obviously it is."

"So why did it only start glowing now? It couldn't have done that before, when we were in all those other situations?" I say to try to break the tension. I look at the jagged blue stone with interest.

"I don't know, but I think it has something to do with the fact that the Lochaere is made up of the stone from the Akmunster Mountains," Wren replies.

"What does that have to do with anything?" I ask in confusion.

"It's said that the mountains were made by light entities and have magical properties, specifically against witches."

Quinn shakes his head. "First dark creatures, then witches, and now this?"

Wren blows a strand of hair out of her face. "There's a lot we don't even know about. King Alberich banished even the thought of magic from people's minds."

"But how?" Zayne asks.

"Now that's a question worth finding the answer to," Wren says thoughtfully.

"How do we get out of here?" Quinn asks after a pause.

I answer, "The same way we got here, I'm guessing."

CHAPTER 27

QUINN

I FEEL LIKE I should be angry that she didn't tell us, but I can't bring myself to be. After all, I'm hiding worse secrets. Secrets that would destroy them.

We finally make it out of the Gardens and I smile in relief. Being the Black Assassin couldn't have prepared me for that. I'm just glad it's over. A slight breeze washes over us. I have no idea how much time passed while we were in there. Based on the temperature and the sunrise, it looks to now be early morning. We discover a small clearing with fallen logs and decide to stop here to eat. I'm starving. As we sit down on the felled trunks, I break some bread and pass it around.

"So how does the plant work?" Zayne asks her.

"It's actually pretty simple."

She retrieves the flower from her bag and plucks three leaves off its stem. "Keep it on your person at all times. If you lose it, tell me and I'll give you another one. We have to do this until I can have time to make a drink containing the plant so we don't have to carry the leaves all the time."

She hands them to us and I rub my thumb against the soft surface. I put it in my pocket.

"Now what?" Zayne asks.

"We have to head to the Kingdom of Elrea. We need to find the other half of the stone as soon as possible," I offer up.

Wren nods in agreement and Zayne looks at his feet. Wren glances at him. "Didn't you tell me that your family lives in the Kingdom of Elrea?"

My ears perk up. This I didn't know.

Zayne lets out a heavy sigh. "Yes. You should probably know this if you want to keep a low profile while you're in the kingdom; you shouldn't hang around with me. It's too dangerous. My father's a rich man, and there are many people who don't like him. Many people who, if they have the opportunity, would use me for ransom. I'm only safe on my father's grounds. All the other times, I have to keep my identity a secret."

I let out a low whistle. "He must be pretty rich if you're that concerned."

Zayne gives me look that says 'you have no idea' and I smirk.

We slowly start making our way to the Kingdom of Elrea. Because we lost our horses some time ago, we are drastically slower, but we try to make up for it by taking fewer breaks. We stop to rest one night and find a place within cover of the forest. Despite its being Autumn, the humid air nudges us to remove our jackets, and we lay them next to us. I have learned a great deal about Wren and Zayne these past few days and it's nice. I never get a chance to talk to people in such a way or get to know them like this.

I learn that Zayne has an older brother and a younger sister, as well as that Wren apparently has a lot of knowledge about herbs. I know that I am taking more time than usual on this mission, but hopefully Damien won't deign it punishable, because what he asks of me is huge. I need to find out a plan fast if I can't bring myself to kidnap Wren. We wish each other a good night, and I lie down on a path of dry ground and stare up at the stars. All of this remains surreal. Like something from a fairytale. Well, I guess, technically, it is part of a fairytale. I never knew there would be so much of the world that people don't know about. I shudder at the thought of how others would react if they knew.

I wake up later in the night at the sound of leaves rustling. The night air is still, and everything appears frozen in time. I start to imagine that I haven't heard anything at all and, with a flutter, my eyes close again. But the moment sleep once again lulls me into its grasp, I hear the same leaves rustling. I open my eyes with a jerk and sit up. I look around but see nothing. Wren lies asleep on the other side of the small clearing, and Zayne is leaning against a rock, keeping watch. He fingers the necklace that he had given Wren for the spell back in that town. With it free of his neck, resting in his hand, he stares at it intently, his eyes hazed with a faraway look.

I gingerly make my way to him, careful to avoid the sticks and stones on the ground so I don't injure my bare feet. He looks up as I approach and slips the necklace back around his throat. He tucks it under his white pirate-like shirt and scoots over when I grow near. I sit next to him, looking out at the fire.

"I can keep watch now," I offer.

He shakes his head. "I can't sleep anyway."

There's a moment of silence as we stare at the dark nothingness around us.

"You're hiding something," he whispers so quietly, I almost don't catch it. "You think I don't know, but I do. You may have Wren fooled, but not me. The way you disappeared somewhere in that town before we headed to the Gardens, and that look that is constantly in your eyes. I know that look; I've seen it on many men's faces. It's the look of a man hiding something. I'm not threatening you; we all have our secrets. But if you bring danger to us, if you are a threat, don't think I will hesitate before I run you through with my sword."

I open my mouth to protest, but he glances at me with tired eyes.

"Do not waste breath," he warns.

I shut my mouth and shock rattles through me. He's smart, smarter than I initially thought. And oddly enough, I feel a sudden respect for him. I hear a voice, and my head whips around once more, again on alert. I squint at the shadows dancing around the clearing.

"Did you hear that?"

Zayne looks at me with confusion. "Hear what?"

"That voice." Because of my training, I can hear sounds that others usually can't detect.

He shakes his head, but before he can say anything, I hear the voice again, this time closer.

Zayne's eyes widen. "I hear it."

Slowly, we get up and move toward the disturbance. We

wait a few seconds before it meets our ears once more, but this time, it sounds like a person singing. I try to catch the words but fail. We take a few more steps forward, and out of the corner of my eye, I see a wisp of white. I turn and watch it disappear behind a tree. I approach the tree and Zayne follows behind me as he unsheathes his sword. I bend down and silently take out the dagger that I had tucked into my boot. We pass the tree - and what I see takes my breath away.

Standing there in the middle of the clearing is a girl who looks like she's around our age, except her features aren't human. She wears an angelic, pearl-white gown and her golden hair is let down to surround her face like a halo. She resembles every bit of an angel. Looking at us, she continues singing. Her words envelop me, and caution seeps out of my body immediately.

Come closer, she sings.

Zayne and I lower our weapons. All conscious thought evaporates as we finally get so near to her that if she reaches her hand out, she can touch us. She halts singing and her gaze on us becomes more intense.

All of a sudden, pain spreads through my body and I start sweating. Zayne is in the same condition and falls to the ground in pain. Clarity suddenly shines in my mind, and I realize how stupid this was. I have a feeling of a thousand knives stabbing me all over, and rational thought escapes me until all I can think about is pain. My view goes blurry, and I see another shadow at the far reaches of my vision. The shadow moves closer, near enough that I can tell it is a person. I close my eyes and I hear the sound of silver and an ear-piercing scream.

At once, I feel a cold breeze wash over me. Immediately, the pain disappears, and I let out a sigh of relief. I feel a hand on my shoulder and roll onto my back. Staring at me, with those gray eyes filled with concern, is Wren. Seeing that I'm all right, she moves to Zayne, and touches his shoulder as well. He gives a low groan, and we lay on the ground for a while until we get the energy to move. I slowly get up, and Zayne does the same. I finally look at Wren and see sweat gleaming on her forehead. She takes a deep breath and turns to us.

"Who lost his leaf?" She wipes her sweat away with the back of her hand.

Zayne reaches into his pocket and takes out the leaf. "Have mine."

They both look at me. "Quinn?" Wren asks.

I shake my head and reach into my jacket– My jacket. I took it off before I slept for the night. I resist the urge to slap my forehead. Stupid. I cringe. "It's in my jacket."

Wren frowns. "Your jacket? You guys could have died!" she says in anger. I feel a twinge of guilt.

"Wren," Zayne says gently but firmly. "He made a mistake, we all do. It's okay, we're fine."

Wren pinches her nose with her ring finger and thumb. She glances at me. "He's right. I- I'm sorry."

"No, it's my fault," I whisper. "I should have worn my jacket."

Zayne's eyes move back and forth between us. Finally, he says, "It's no one's fault. Someone was bound to lose or forget their leaf. It just happened to be Quinn."

CHAPTER 28

ZAYNE

THE NEXT MORNING, we get up and continue like nothing happened. We are packing our things and I'm shoving my gray blanket into my bag when Wren blurts, "I need to see someone before we go to the kingdom, if you guys don't mind. It's on our way there, and we can get more supplies as well."

I shrug. "That's fine. But we're running out of time. We should hurry up. Who is it?"

"Someone who knew my mother. There's something of my mother's that I need there," she replies. She looks at Quinn. "Are you fine with us making a quick stop?"

Quinn nods. "Of course."

By this time, we are deep in the forest, and as we walk, we start to hear the sound of rushing water.

"We should find where that water is coming from," Wren says as her head perks up.

I look at her, confused. "We have enough water."

She shakes her head. "I need somewhere to make the potion that will conceal us from the Sorcerer. And there's a specific juice of a fruit that's relatively easy to find, but it's only found near running water."

Quinn leans toward the noise and starts walking to it. Wren and I look at each other before we follow him. We carefully make our way around foliage, and Quinn finally leads us to the source of the noise. Wren slips her bag off of her shoulder and settles on a rock near the stream. The stream in question isn't as wide as I thought it would be, but it is by no means small. The dirty water washes over rocks with force as it makes its way downstream.

I glance at Wren and sit on a giant rock next to her. Quinn joins me and we both look at Wren in curiosity. She takes out some tiny vials containing herbs and things I recognize from the shop we stopped by. Finally, she takes out the plant, and we all hold our breath.

Wren looks at both of us. "Do you guys have a cloth or something I could lay on the ground to set this all out on?"

"I think I have something," I respond. I reach into my bag and take out a red stretch of fabric.

Wren reaches out her hand and thanks me as I hand it to her. She gently plucks three petals off of the flower and those petals' glow dims immediately.

"Zayne, can you check the banks of the stream for a small fruit? It's pretty tiny and purple. It'll have green thorns growing out of the stems and it lies close to the ground."

I get up slowly. "This better be easy to find," I mutter.

"What is that?" Wren asks and I jump.

"Nothing."

I walk toward the bank and I groan when I see many items in the shade of purple. I start with a purple cluster of berries on my right. I kneel down and check, but see that there are no thorns. I go through tall flowers with thorns, flowers without thorns, plants with thorns, but nothing fits Wren's description. I'm about to give up, and turn around to tell Wren that there's nothing, when I glimpse something apart from all the other plants and fruit. Hovering slightly above the grass is a small diamond-shaped fruit with the tips reaching toward the sky. Its light purple hue sparkles against the sky. I grin when I see the small thorn protruding from the stem. Making sure that I don't cut my fingers, I carefully pluck the flower from the ground.

I hurry toward Wren, and when I reach her, I raise the fruit slightly. "Is this it?"

Wren looks up and grins. "I can't believe you actually found it. It only pops up here and there. There were a lot before King Alberich's time. Before he banished magic."

"So, you're telling me, I could have been running all over this place for a fruit that may have not been here?"

She gives a sheepish smile. "But you found it."

I roll my eyes and take my seat next to Quinn again. "Could have helped me," I mutter.

Quinn gives a low laugh. "Looked like you were taking care of it."

"How gracious of you."

We fall silent as Wren collects the flower petals and

gently crushes them with a rock she must have found while I was gone. She places the crushed remains into a small wooden bowl and adds some herbs. Finally, she takes the purple fruit and presses hard. Immediately, its soft skin breaks gently and a green, sticky liquid seeps into the bowl. Suddenly, a foul smell hits me and I gag.

I hold my fist to my mouth and groan. "What's that horrid smell?"

Quinn looks at me, confused. "What smell?"

Wren snaps her head up. "You can smell it?"

"Unfortunately."

She shakes her head in confusion, and I think I see a glimpse of fear in her eyes.

I slowly lower my hand. "What?"

"On- only people that have supernatural blood can detect the odor."

I feel a chill run down my back. "What?"

Holding my gaze, Wren's eyes are as wide as saucers. Finally, she relaxes. "Maybe you have some blood from a really ancient ancestor. If that's the case, then you don't have any ability with magic, but you might still have it running through you."

I relax. That is probably it. "Interesting," I whisper.

Wren stares at me for a second longer before turning her attention back to the bowl. "Don't worry. We can suffer through the smell together."

I attempt to smile, but the words 'supernatural' and 'blood' still echo through my mind.

I turn to see Quinn watching me with a calm, calculating look in his eyes. I frown and return my gaze to the bowl, trying to ignore the expression - a look that says he thinks I can be a threat.

The smell progresses to get worse and, just when I think I can't bear it anymore, then the smell is gone. Instead, it is replaced with a sweet aroma that reminds me of the honey my siblings and I would sneak to our rooms from the kitchen. I lean over to see the concoction that Wren has made and Quinn does the same. We look into the bowl and I cringe when I see a dirty, brown liquid.

"We have to drink that?" Quinn says with disgust.

"Unless you want to go through the town incident again," Wren says, quirking an eyebrow.

She pours the liquid into similar wooden cups that she has in her bag, a little into each. She pours the excess liquid into a bigger jar that she puts into our satchel. "We have to drink small amounts at a time. Too much at once is toxic."

She hands us the cup, and we all uneasily look at the thick substance within. The honey smell has faded into almost nothing. We quickly knock back the drinks, and I try not to gag at the taste of the liquid sliding down my throat. It tastes like ash and tar at the same time. I flinch and wait until the taste disappears, but it doesn't. The taste still lingers on my tongue. Wren holds the cup far from herself and makes a sour face.

"That was atrocious."

"How often do we have to take this, exactly?" Quinn asks after a brief silence.

"From what my mother told me, it's once a day."

"Odd. It feels like your mother knew what information you would need."

Wren rubs her neck. "I think she knew there was a possibility something could go wrong. She was the type of person who would think of everything."

"Hopefully it wasn't all for nothing," I say.

CHAPTER 29

QUINN

IT'S AN ODD feeling: the sensation of inferiority. I know it's silly, and even though Zayne doesn't actually have any active magic - that we know of – and I'm an assassin, I can't help but feel threatened now that I'm surrounded by two people who have magic in their veins. Even though for one, that magic is dormant.

The next day, Wren leads us instead of me. I showed Wren the map earlier and showed her exactly where we are so that she knows how to find what her mother left her. Wren leads us out of the forest and onto a dirt path; the forest soon fades away into green plains. It was not long after we stepped on the path that a wagon passes us. Sitting on the seat is an old man wearing a red vest over a white button-down shirt. He's wearing loose, old brown pants that look too big for him, and on his feet are worn-out, brown, goatskin shoes. He gives us an odd look but doesn't stop. What a sight we must be, a couple of teenagers that are dirty and exhausted from a long journey he couldn't even fathom. He's the first person we've seen in a while.

"We're almost to the Kingdom of Elrea," Zayne says with a start.

Wren smiles. "Great. We can stop by the gypsy camp and then make our way. How long is it from here to the kingdom?"

"A day alm-" Zayne starts, but then shakes his head. "Did you just say gypsy camp?"

"They don't welcome outsiders, Wren. You know that," I say, confused.

"That's the thing. I'm not an outsider," she reveals. "This is the camp my mother's from. They are always moving, but are usually here at this time of the year. If we're lucky, we can catch them before they leave."

Wren's mother was a gypsy? I put aside this information and ask, "But what about us? We're outsiders."

Wren bites her lip in worry. "I guess we can just hope that they welcome all of us. They might not even let me in."

"Why not? Your mother was from there," Zayne asks.

Wren shrugs. "I have a feeling."

Something within me says there is more to the story, but I don't ask. Maybe we'll know what she's talking about when we reach the gypsy camp.

In wonder, I realize that even though, as an assassin, I got to see many places, this journey consists of places I never thought I would visit.

As we continue walking, I look into the distance and catch a glimpse of the castle of Elrea in the distance. I remember going to Elrea before for missions and I remember it being a beautiful place, but, like everywhere else, I soon realized that under the façade, there is a darkness in which felons, murderers, and thieves thrive. Still, compared to the places I've been, I wouldn't mind going back there at all.

I am so lost in my thoughts that I don't realize Wren and Zayne have stopped. I shake out of my ponderings and look at them, confused.

"Why did we stop?" I ask.

"We're here."

I look around, but all I see are the plains surrounding us. A gentle wind stirs the grass and kisses my face as I take a deep breath of the sweet smell from the flowers. If I wasn't forever tied to the Compound in servitude, then I wouldn't mind staying here. There's something about this place untouched by the greed of men and war.

Wren points to a hill. "It's just over that hill. There's a valley there where they probably are." If they are at all.

Wren adjusts her satchel and starts walking toward the hill. Zayne and I exchange a knowing look before following her. Our feet leave soft imprints in the grass that disappear seconds later. I look up to the sky that seems to be growing darker by the second and absentmindedly hope that it doesn't rain. We'll be enveloped in it if there's no camp, and I hope there is, for Wren's sake. As we near the top of the hill, I watch as Wren's face becomes more and more anxious. I watch her expression as she reaches the top of the hill; I watch it turn into a look of elation and I relax.

They are here. Zayne and I catch up to her and look down at the scene below us. Down in the valley are small flickering lights, as well as many caravans and tens of different colors. Smoke rises from what seems like a fire in the middle of the camp. I softly smile; I've never been to a gypsy camp. I see Wren take a quick step forward, but I stop her with my hand. I look into her eyes to make sure she understands what I'm about to say next.

"You don't know if it's them. Be careful."

She hesitates but finally nods. I let her go, and we all start making it down the hill more carefully. By now, the sky has grown darker, and the air has filled with the sounds of nightlife. Just as we're about to approach the camp, I hear a rustling of leaves and I stop. It could just be the wind, but we can't take any chances. I gesture for Zayne and Wren to stop, and they do so in confusion. I squint at the shadows before us, and my eyes widen as I see a silhouette. Realizing that it's been spotted, the shadow steps out into the light. It's a woman. Her brown hair is streaked with gray, and lines of wariness are etched into her face. Her green eyes are narrowed at us with suspicion, and as I look around, I realize that no one is with her.

"What is your business here?" A heavy accent tilts her voice and I have to concentrate to understand what she is saying.

Wren steps up. "We are here to see Dika."

The woman's eyes bunch together. "How did you hear her name?"

"My mother."

"And who is your mother, young one?"

"Maria."

The woman's face pales and she takes a step back. "That

is why you look so familiar." There is a brief silence before she continues, "What is your business here?"

"We are here to see Dika," Wren replies once again.

The woman sighs. "You will not tell me, fine. We do not let outsiders in, but if you are Maria's daughter…" She shakes her head. "We will see what Dika says. There is a small chance she will let you stay, but I don't know about those two." She jerks her head at Zayne and me. Her gaze lingers on Zayne, and for a second I think her eyes fill with confusion, but it disappears as soon as it came.

Wren looks at us, and we nod back at her. "That is fine," she replies.

The woman smiles and says, "You look just like your mother."

Wren's eyes fill with sadness. "Thank you."

She starts walking back into the camp, and we rush to follow her.

"What are your names?" she asks. Wren tells her and she nods. "I am Vadoma. I-"

Before she can finish her sentence, however, a tiny squeal fills the air and a small blur of red sprints forward, hugging her legs. I realize it's a child. A girl, in fact. The girl herself seems to be around five, and she has soft, curly, brown hair and green eyes like Vadoma.

Vadoma laughs. "And this is my grand-daughter, Mirella." Mirella looks at us, fascinated by the strangers. Wren gives her a small wave, and Mirella slowly walks up to her and holds her hand. Vadoma laughs once again. "She likes you."

CHAPTER 30

WREN

THE GYPSY CAMP is even more beautiful up close. They have hung up small lanterns everywhere, and they wear colorful garments. It is unlike anything I have ever seen. Mirella pulls me along by my arm with a smile on her face. Her tiny hand squeezes mine tightly, as if I would disappear when she let go. She leads me along the grass, and I smile. Even the tents are in different shades.

There are many caravans, and we see various people milling around. The moon above shines silver on everything around us. Mirella leads me to the huge tent in the center of camp, and she enters in a rush, pulling me with her. We pass through a beaded curtain, and my breath escapes me. There are bursts of color, everywhere. There are cushions on the floor, and people mill around happily, talking over the clacking of wooden glasses and plates.

I'm aware of Quinn and Zayne as they enter the tent,

but I don't look back. Mirella leads me through the people who fall silent as they spy the three strangers in their midst. Mirella, oblivious to the stares, leads me through the people as they part for us. Finally, she stops and I halt to a stop next to her. I realize we are standing in front of a woman in her mid-sixties. She has beads and ribbons in her hair, with icy blue eyes currently narrowed at us. I feel Zayne and Quinn's presence behind me.

After a brief silence, the woman finally speaks cuttingly and asks, "What is this, Vadoma?" Like Vadoma, she has an accent. Gypsies don't like anyone who that's not like them.

Vadoma steps up. "I found these three just outside the camp, Dika. They claim to have come all the way from the Kingdom of Ulalle. They've had a long journey and I offered them a place to stay here for a while. They can stay in my tent."

Dika frowns. "We don't tolerate strangers."

"Sister, please. They need to rest."

I raise my eyebrows in surprise. Vadoma and Dika are sisters.

"No, and that is final."

I whisper to Vadoma, "Is it okay if I say something?"

She looks at me with caution. "Be careful with what comes out of your mouth, child." But she nods.

I step up and say, "I am a Reinecourt." That's my surname. I hear gasps at the name, but I ignore them.

Dika straightens immediately. "What did you say?"

"Please let us stay for just a while. We'll be gone before

daybreak. I need something of my mother's, and we will be on our way."

Sadness, anger, and guilt show on Dika's face. "No. Your mother turned her back on her own and married a man that isn't from our clans."

"She loved him and, because of it, you kicked her out." I say this with some edge in my tone. Guilt flicks across her features quickly, but it is gone in the blink of an eye. "And now she's dead." My voice cracks a little.

Sorrow washes over her. "She was my best friend." She looks up. "I've done things I shouldn't have done, and the least I can do is let her daughter stay for a while," Dika says as she looks at her sister and sighs. "Very well, but you are responsible for them."

Vadoma softly replies, "Of course." She quickly smiles and turns to us. She looks at me with new-found interest and deep sorrow. "You all must be hungry. Please come."

She walks outside without looking back and we all follow her, Mirella included. The little girl is still holding my hand as we walk up to another tent, smaller than the one we just left. It is blue, in a shade that much reminds me of the sea. Once again, there are beads hanging in the entrance, and they clink as we pass. I immediately smell food and spices, and my mouth waters.

"We are grateful for your kindness," Quinn tells her gently.

She waves his words away as if they're nothing.

"Truly, thank you," I add.

She smiles. "This world is full of war and hatred. Without kindness, we aren't human."

Vadoma motions for us to sit on an arrangement of cushions, and she walks to a pot that I'm sure is the source of the mouthwatering smell. She picks up some bowls and pours stew into them. Steam rises from the bowls as she hands them to us. "Many thanks," I whisper. She puts a bowl in front of Mirella, who is sitting right next to me.

She chuckles. "She has grown fond of you already."

I grin. "She's beautiful."

"I know," Vadoma says with a smile, looking at her grand-child fondly. She steps back and then runs an appraising look over us. "You all must be in a hurry." Zayne, Quinn, and I glance at each other. She notices and shakes her head, saying, "Don't worry. I don't ask questions. But stay tomorrow. Please. I knew your mother well. Your mother, Dika, and I were very close. I can't believe her daughter is sitting in front of me."

I start shaking my head, but Quinn puts a hand on my arm. "Yes, we can stay. Zayne and I agree that you should, Wren."

I look at them in shock. "But-"

Zayne looks at me with soft eyes. "We can tell this is important to you, Wren."

Shocked, I smile at them. I can't believe they're willing to give up valuable time for me. I grin and look at Vadoma. "Okay. If it's not too much trouble."

She shakes her head quickly. "No, not at all. I'll talk to Dika."

Zayne and Quinn are shown to a tent they can stay in, and Vadoma tells me I can rest here while she and her grand-daughter sleep in their wagon. I quickly insist that they should stay in the tent, but Vadoma shoots me down by explaining they are used to sleeping in their wagon. She leaves the tent then, and I quickly change into more comfortable clothing.

The next morning, Zayne and Quinn help gather wood from the forest. When I offer to do something as well, they explain they have dishes I could help with, but I shake my head at the task. I offer to hunt for them, but before I can leave, a woman arrives and tells that Dika has called for me. The woman explains that she is in the large tent, and then leaves. I enter the tent and I spot Dika sitting on one of the cushions. The rest of the tent is empty. She looks up as I enter and gestures for me sit down next to her. I hesitate for a second before relenting.

"I knew your mother more than anyone. She would tell me everything." She smiles but I don't say anything. She continues after a brief silence. "Which is why I know about your magic."

She glances at me from the corner of her eye. I whip my head up. "What?" We don't tell anyone. Ever.

"As the chief, I have to kindly ask you not to use your magic on our grounds." I nod and she continues. "We move camp in another three days, so you must leave by then. But, I heard that you're leaving before then anyway." She pauses and then sighs. "You're not saying anything."

I shrug and finally look at her. "What do you want me to say? My aunt told me what you did to my mother."

"What I did was wrong, and I regret it. I don't expect you to forgive me, but know that I'm deeply sorry."

Those are words. It doesn't justify what she did, and I

know I won't ever forgive, but I don't hate her. I understand why she did it, but that doesn't mean it was the right thing to do.

"My mother. Before she- she died…" The words leave a sour taste in my mouth, but I continue, "She said she left me something from the place she was born."

Dika looks at me for a long time before finally saying, "I know what you're talking about." She sighs and gets up.

I scramble up to my feet and look at her. "Really?"

She smiles a little. "Yes, really. She found out that we had set up camp near here and she came back a week after you were born, despite being banished. No one else knows this. I can't let people think that I'm not a leader who sticks by the rules. She left a small box for you. I let her have one last request, and she asked for me to keep it safe and for no one except you to look at it unless you chose for them to see it. She told me that it would be safe here."

Excitement shoots through me. "Well, where is it?" I ask with eagerness.

She opens her mouth to answer, but before she can say anything, a man strides in. "Dika, there is an emergency. One of the tents caught on fire."

"What? Then what are you waiting for? Get water and douse it!"

"People are doing just that, right at this moment."

Dika relaxes slightly, but the tension in her muscles is still apparent. She glances at me. "Come with me. I will show you what you desire after we take care of this little problem."

Impatience threatens to take over, but I quickly shove it down. I've waited this long. I can wait a little longer. We hurry out of the tent, and immediately I smell smoke. I look around and see a pillar of blackness rising into the air. We walk toward it until a burning tent appears.

"Was there anyone in the tent when the fire started?"

"No. We asked some people nearby if they saw anyone enter, and they said that they didn't," a man says.

"Good. Cause?" Dika asks.

He shakes his head. "Unknown."

Dika spends a little more time asking questions, but soon the fire is extinguished and everyone gets bored, continuing with their tasks from before the fire. I glance around and frown when I see a circular patch of burnt grass next to the tent. How odd…

Dika approaches me, and I focus on her with hope in my eyes. She sees my face and exhales. "Yes, come with me. I'll show you what you're looking for."

Before I can help it, I feel hope to finally see the object my mom used to guard with her life. We walk past some children chasing each other, and everyone is about, doing chores, creating the feeling of community. My mother would tell me many stories of this place, and now I can tell why she shared them with love. This place is filled with people who work together, and everyone is family. It's beautiful. We arrive at one of the gitanes, slightly bigger than the rest of them, and Dika glances at me.

She gestures to the wagon with her head. "Climb in," she says.

I hesitate before doing as she instructs. The second I

enter, I notice lanterns here and there, and Dika moves to light them. Blankets and pillows lie around, and in the corner is a small chest. Dika walks toward the chest while reaching up and lifting a necklace from under her blouse. I didn't notice it until now. A silver key that is worn with age hangs from the black, twisted string. I hold my breath as Dika inserts the key into a golden keyhole. A small click resonates through the wagon as I move closer. She removes the key and hands the necklace to me. "You can do as you want with this. I don't need it anymore."

She gives me a nod and leaves the wagon so I have privacy. I slowly approach the chest and kneel in front of it. I lift my hand up and wipe at the thick layer of dust coating the façade. I clean my hand on my gown and slowly push the lid off the chest. It resists at first, but then finally gives in with a rasp. I slowly peer inside and take a sharp breath as my eyes see a tiny silver box at the bottom of the chest. Small blue jewels ornate the box, and in the middle is the same elegant symbol, now blue, of a triangle with the arrow going through it.

I don't know how, but somehow this symbol is a big part of everything. Gently, I remove the box from the chest and carefully set it on my lap. I flip the small latch with my index finger, and the world seems to fade to black as I open the lid and finally see what my mother held dear to her heart. With barely held excitement, I see a book. The world screeches to a halt.

A book? I look closer and slowly realize that it's the children's book my mother used to read to me when I was little. The words Fairytales and Ancient Lore glisten in gold against the black leather cover. Maybe- maybe she wrote something in it? A spell? I quickly pick up the worn book and flip through the yellowed pages. My hope deflates quickly as I look at page after page. Nothing. No notes. I flip to the last page and my heart stops when I see my mother's handwriting.

Confusion fills me. Why did she leave me this? Still… it's one of the last things I have of her. I hug it to my chest and leave the wagon.

The rest of the day, I help around the camp and catch only glimpses of Quinn and Zayne. I finally meet up with them during dinner. We stand in a line to get stew and make small talk.

"So, what did you guys do all day?" I ask them.

"We helped get wood for the most part," Quinn says. He glances at Zayne with humor. "Or at least I did. This guy here, well-"

"What do you mean by that?" Zayne asks with a laugh as he shakes his head.

I snort loudly. They both look at me, startled, and then we all burst into laughter.

Some people around us stare curiously, and others smile. We finally get our food and sit on wooden logs near the main fire. The embers fly around as we dig into the stew in wooden bowls. Other gypsies soon join us and I notice a group of children nearby.

One of them shouts, "Ludia, you promised to tell us a story!" I see a middle-aged woman smile, and she gestures for the children to sit down in front of her in the grass. They comply and move in a rush.

"What is the story today?" another woman asks Ludia, chuckling.

Ludia laughs. "This time it's one of the outsiders' famous stories."

A gentle wind blows then, stirring her hair. In a weird way, it sets the atmosphere and even I lean forward, interested in what she is about to say.

"This story is one of magic and loss and new beginnings. And it would be best if I started from the beginning. There once was a girl. She loved her parents very much and her parents loved her just as much. They were gone for long periods of time and she stayed with her aunt, but the moments they spent together were forever treasured in her heart."

I lean back as my heart clenches. I know this story. It's my story. Quinn and Zayne recognize it too and they stiffen. I see them glance at me from the corner of my eyes, but they say nothing. I stare at the fire as Ludia continues.

"She grew up and, when she was old enough, her parents told her what they did when they were gone. They told her about adventures with magic and darkness. They told her that she herself had magic, like them, and that they used their magic to protect others. In secret, they started teaching her magic and spells, and her aunt helped. They did this in secret, for there were those who would call them witches and persecute them. The girl requested to go with her parents every time they left. But they refused, saying it was too dangerous and she wasn't ready yet. One day, as she was walking through the house after a nightmare, she caught sight of her mother turning a corner. She followed her silently, curious as to what she was up to in the middle of the night, and she followed her to the back of the cottage and to the door her parents never let her open. The girl peeked around the corner and watched as her mother quietly opened the door to reveal her father already waiting on the other side.

"'What are we going to do with it, Philip?' her mother asked her father.

"Her father replied, 'There's no other option but to destroy it.' Her mother nodded and her father said, 'It might not work, Maria.'

"'I know,' said the girl's mother, and as they both stepped aside, the girl caught sight of an onyx box with a symbol of a triangle with an arrow through it. The girl stepped back. It was the exact same box that was in her nightmares."

Zayne clenches his hand and whispers, "That's the sign that was on the bodies."

"The Enchanters' Child was confused on what was happening, and she knew she wasn't supposed to be there. Curiosity, however, got the best of her, and she stayed where she was. Her parents held each other's hands, and Philip gave Maria a reassuring squeeze. They turned to face the box as they started muttering words. The box started glowing a golden hue. And then silence. The Enchanters relaxed with smiles on their faces, but they didn't notice the black shadow slowly rising its way out of the box. The girl screamed in warning, but it was too late. As the Enchanters swirled toward the box in horror, the black shadow crashed into them. The girl shut her eyes until the screams stopped; tears were running down her face. Finally, when there was silence, she opened her eyes to see her parents and the box gone."

I flinch and memories flash in my mind. I remember that day like it just happened. The deadly silence of the house when I woke from my nightmare of a shadow and a box. The creaking of the floorboards as I moved through the cottage, looking for my parents when I didn't find them in their bedroom.

"Later, the girl found out the shadow was a person from her aunt. The shadow was called the Sorcerer. The Enchanters' Child is the world's last hope. The last person left with light magic, and the weight of the world was then forever on her shoulders."

The words rattle and echo through my head. *And the weight of the world was then forever on her shoulders.* If I fail-

I stop myself before I finish that thought. I won't fail. I can't.

"What happens next? How does it end?" one of the children asks breathlessly.

Ludia smiles. "Well, that's up to you. What do you think?" she asks with a twinkle in her eyes.

"Good wins," the child says confidently. I smile a little at this and the other children quickly agree, shouting their different endings.

Ludia grins and then gestures for the children to quiet down. Almost immediately, they do so. They lean forward expectantly and Ludia drops her voice an octave for effect. "They say that the Enchanters' Child is healthy, alive, and among us, waiting to make her move and defeat the Sorcerer and his wicked ways. They say that she's been biding her time, practicing her magic, and becoming stronger and more powerful than even her parents were."

At the last sentence, I scoff. *Right, I wish.* I huddle into my thin, yet warm, woven jacket. Soon, the children run off the chase each other and I watch them laugh and giggle as one of the girls chases after the boys. An unexpected wave of sadness washes over me. I miss my parents.

CHAPTER 31

ZAYNE

HESITANTLY, I LOOK at Wren after Ludia finishes the story. It must have been hard, hearing all of that. I look at her and see sadness I can't even begin to fathom shining in her eyes. She stares at the ground and it looks as if she wishes it could swallow her up. In her hand, she clutches the book that she's been carrying around all day in a tight grip and her knuckles turn white. I sigh and share a glance with Quinn before getting up and slowly walking to her.

I stop a foot away. "Hey."

Wren takes a shuddering breath and looks up. She blinks a few tears away and finally gives me a gentle smile.

"Will you walk with me?" I ask her.

She gets up. "I need to walk around anyway."

We trek for a while until the sounds of the camp are muted. We walk between wagons and tents, making a circle around the camp. "Did you find what you were look-ing for?" I ask as I try to cheer her up.

Her eyebrows pull together. "Yes, but it isn't what I expected."

I glance at her quickly. "What do you mean?"

"She gave me a copy of the book she used to read to me when I was little."

"And?"

"I don't know." She kicks a pebble on the pathway. "I just thought I would find something to help us."

I take a slow breath in and hope she doesn't hate me for what I'm about to say. Someone has to tell her. "I realize how important defeating the Sorcerer is to you, to all of us, but I feel like you're so wrapped up in revenge that you're not letting yourself loosen up. You are not enjoying your life. Your parents wouldn't want this for you."

She stops abruptly, and in a cold voice says, "You have no idea what my parents would want."

"Defeating the Sorcerer is to make the world a better place," I persist. "I realize what he's done to you. I don't completely understand, I never will, and I'm not telling you to not hate him and not to make him pay for what he's done. But, Wren, this has followed you for all your life. I pity you that instead of looking at the book and seeing the sentimental value that your mother has given to you, you feel disappointment."

She flinches like I slapped her across the face, and she take a slow step back. "You have no right. None."

Her face is grim, and she turns and walks away, leaving me behind.

The only noise is the chirping of the crickets and the slight breeze in the air. I feel immense sadness for her immediately. Hopefully, one day she'll realize the value of what I said. I want her to live her life and enjoy it, not always looking behind her back and being filled with revenge and hate.

The next early morning, I'm woken by the sound of feet shuffling inside the tent. I freeze, acting like I'm asleep, and wait with bated breath. What is someone doing in my tent?

"I know you are awake, young one," says a soft voice, and I whip open my eyes before I sit up. As my eyes adjust, I make out a figure next to the opening of the tent.

"Vadoma?" I ask curiously.

"Come," she says, and then she turns and starts walking out of the tent.

Confused and shocked, I hurry to follow her. The cool air of the night stings my skin and awakens me as I breathe it in. The moon bathes everything in a white glow and helps me find Vadoma in the darkness. She continues walking and doesn't stop until we are at the edge of camp. A small river cuts through the grass, and the trickling water is the only sound in the otherwise desolate night. Vadoma approaches the stream and casually sits down on the banks.

As I draw closer, I slowly become aware of the situation and glare at her. For all I know, this could be a trap. I fold my arms across my chest and widen my stance. "Why have you brought me out here?"

"Patience," she chides, and shoots me a disapproving look.

An uncomfortable silence hangs in the air, and I unconsciously shuffle my feet. Finally, she breaks the silence, but what she says next makes fear shoot through me. "I know you started the fire."

"Wh- what?"

"The fire? Tent?" she says slowly, like I didn't hear her the first time.

I gulp. "I don't know what you're talking about."

"It's pointless lying to me. I saw you."

She looks at me, and I must seem panicked because she says, "Don't worry. I can help you."

I squint at her. "How?"

"Have you gotten bursts of something like this before now?"

I think for a second. "No."

She tilts her head. "Think."

"There was this one ti- No, it's stupid."

She leans forward. "You never know."

"There was this one time when a book moved, but I didn't touch it. I can't be sure that it was magic." I almost tell her about my about having dormant magic, but I don't want to reveal so much to an almost total stranger.

"You have magic, Zayne. I think magic that's been dormant since you were born because of no training. But it's starting to awaken again. You mustn't tell anyone until you are sure. You can't protect yourself with magic yet and that leaves you very vulnerable. The protection you can find is only with people with magic like yours. But there are none anymore, I'm afraid. Be careful, and if you do happen to know someone with knowledge of this magic, you must let them train you."

I open my mouth to argue, but she gives me a look that tells me to wait. I shut my mouth, but when I look down at my hands, I realize that I'm shaking. Little did she know that Wren was one of those people. Confusion and fear rushes through me, along with numerous other feelings I don't have time to decipher. "I don't want this. I didn't ask for this."

Vadoma shakes her head. "What you have is a gift. Don't think of it as a curse. But gifts like this do come with consequences, so you must be cautious with people. People fear things they do not understand and fear can make people do unspeakable things."

Panic claws its way through me, and I clench my eyes shut in an attempt to somehow stop the truth from reaching me. I have a sudden flashback to earlier that day.

I walk around camp, thinking about my family. Especially my sister. Despite the risks, I'll have to make an attempt to see her before we leave Elrea. I take in the people working around me as a group of children chase each other. Oddly, they remind me of when I was little. Being rich, many people tried to get close to my family. All relationships were built with lies. It wasn't until I became the captain of the guard for the Kingdom of Elrea that I made true friends in the soldiers around me. We had a true bond that I didn't have with anyone else, except one.

When I was little, I remember always playing with one girl. For some reason, my father let me spend time with her; he usually forbids me from making friends because of the danger of people using me to gain things for themselves. The girl and I, we would create imaginary worlds and escape into them for as long as possible before her parents told her that she had to leave. She disappeared when I was young, so she wasn't in my life long, but she stays in my memories. She was the closest thing to a friend that I had for many years, until I grew up.

I jolt back to the present and notice that I am behind a tent and there are no people around. I close my eyes to try to preserve the peace because I know that, soon, we'll be back on a journey that will end up with death. Hopefully, not on our side.

Worry seeps through me about the journey ahead of us and I absently smell smoke. My eyes fly open. Smoke. I look down at my feet and jump back when I see that the grass is on fire. It quickly spreads to the tent, and before I know it, it is engulfed in fire. I run inside the tent and see that no one is in it. Relief surges through me, and I run to get help.

When I open my eyes, Vadoma is gone. Wren avoids me as we all meet up to leave the camp. Quinn glances between us and senses that something happened, but he says nothing. A handful of gypsies wait for us including Dika, Vadoma, and Mirella.

Vadoma walks up with Mirella holding her hand. She smiles at us and says goodbye individually. When she comes to bid me farewell, she doesn't mention the earlier morning. I feel sudden relief. I need some time to process the information, but I plan to tell Wren soon.

Vadoma moves on to Wren, and Mirella wraps her small

arms halfway around Wren to hug her. Vadoma chuckles. "She's grown fond of you."

Wren smiles. "I'll come back and visit if you guys set up camp here again." She doesn't add what we all are thinking: if she survives. Or maybe it's just me thinking that.

We leave camp and make our way back to the road, after taking another drink of the Glasswitch flower mixture. The Kingdom of Elrea becomes larger, and I think about my father. Hopefully, I can go unnoticed during our trip, and no one will recognize me or tell my father. Quinn and Wren talk to each other ahead of me, and I notice she's purposely avoiding me.

I sigh, knowing I can't do anything about it. As we keep walking, Quinn falls back in line with me, and I see his lips moving but don't register any of the words. I'm too worried about someone knowing my face. When Quinn realizes I'm not listening, he gives me a frown and stops talking. We walk in silence, and then finally enter the kingdom. I let out a sigh of relief that the guards didn't recognize me, but that's also a problem. I trained them myself, but they are obviously doing a bad job when it comes to the security at the gate.

Quinn gives me an odd look and finally speaks up. "Hey, are you okay?"

"Yeah, I'm just relieved to finally be back."

He gives me a doubtful expression. "Really? Because there seems to be more to it. It seems like you're hiding," he says, gesturing at the cloak and hood that now conceal my face.

I give a shrug, hoping that he believes my act of nonchalance.

"There are people who don't like my family," I say sticking to a semblance of the truth.

I can tell that Quinn knows there is more to the story, but he doesn't say anything else. Even Wren glances at me suspiciously, but I shrug it off. Let them judge me. I don't really care. They don't realize how many people would know my face, and I really don't want to make a scene. My father will be outraged that I didn't tell him I was coming. He would probably spin it into a story, about how I'm always looking for attention and how I shouldn't mingle with people 'below' us. Regrettably, I seldom argued with my father. He is a force to be reckoned with. The one time I fought with him was to be captain of the guard, and even that had consequences; I'm not allowed to leave the kingdom unless it's in the call of duty.

We pass a food stand, and Wren's stomach grumbles. She smiles sheepishly. "We should probably eat."

I frown, but as we approach the stand, we are hit with a soft aroma of sweets that cause my mouth to water. The stand itself is meager and the baker stands behind it. Quinn walks up and orders three tarts. I shift on my feet and, abruptly, a passerby slams into me. My hood flies off and I freeze.

I quickly grab the hood and am about to replace it on my head when I see the baker's face. His face is white with shock, and I feel dread.

"Your Highness," says the baker, his eyes wide.

Oh no. Not now, not here in the middle of the street.

CHAPTER 32
QUINN

I TURN IN SHOCK as the baker looks behind me. Things seem to happen in slow motion as Zayne lets the hood hang limp in his hand. Wren takes in a sharp breath and Zayne winces. Confusion fills the air. Only royalty is referred to as, 'Your Highness.' I look around, perplexed, but don't see anyone except us at the stand. The baker nudges past me and bows in front of Zayne.

"This is an honor. Truly," he says.

Shocked, I look on in numb silence.

"The honor is all mine," Zayne replies.

I shake my head; the baker must be mistaken. But then why did Zayne respond like this, as if it were something to be expected?

Suddenly, Zayne's behavior makes more sense. The way he was shocked to hear that the stone was in Elrea. The fact that he comes from a wealthy family, so much so that he is in danger all the time. I run my hand down my face. He is a prince? Our very own Zayne? Understanding hits me. Nicolaus Zayne Ashleigh. I shake my head in amazement. There are few times in my life when I am surprised, but in this instance, I have to admit I didn't see it coming.

I look at Wren and see that she appears even more shocked than I am. Her face is paler than ever, and her eyes are wide. As an assassin, I'm trained to take things in stride, so I try not to dwell on this new surprise. Luckily, one of the guards is here, wearing the forest-green and gold uniforms that are the colors of the kingdom, and he makes his way through the crowd that has begun to form until he finally reaches Zayne.

"Look who is back!" the guard says, grinning.

He has chestnut hair, currently in disarray, and slight wrinkles appear on the edge of his hazel eyes when he smiles.

"Lucas?" Zayne says in surprise.

They laugh and hug for a good minute before Zayne remembers that we exist. He gives us an uncomfortable look.

"Oh, Lucas. This is Quinn and Wren. They're new friends of mine."

As always, I cringe at the word 'friends.' Through this journey, despite all the secrets, we've managed to create a bond. We were broken people who, despite it all, came together. There's no way I'm going to take Wren to Damien. I can't. Can't betray them like that. I'll deal with it later. I'll save my sister some way. The thought of my sister makes my heart stop. She wouldn't be proud of who

I am today. But everything I'm doing is for her. If she's even alive anymore.

Lucas gives us a big grin. "It's nice to meet both of you."

Right away I can tell that he's one of the charming types. It's a weird comfort to know that, even though Zayne kept what he really is from us, at least he doesn't think that everyone else is below him. He's good friends with the soldier, it seems. They must be really good friends if Lucas talks to him so casually.

"We should probably leave before we attract any more attention," Lucas adds.

"I think it's too late for that." Zayne says with a sigh.

We walk down the dirt path, and Lucas keeps looking around for any signs of danger toward the prince. "So where have you been? You're barely here anymore. The guards miss you," he says to Zayne.

"You know how much I like traveling," Zayne says, smiling. But it doesn't reach his eyes. There was more to it. Maybe it's the Gavreel Society or maybe something else.

"I guess. You are always the one who likes adventure," Lucas says, chuckling.

"Yes, my brother's the more responsible one," Zayne says with a smile. But his face turns grim as he adds, "Father hates that I'm not more like him."

Lucas goes quiet and says nothing.

Zayne's the one to break the silence. "How's everything at the palace?"

"Good. Your brother and sister are well, and with the

Autumn Ball in a couple of days, everyone's in a rush to get things prepared."

Zayne smacks his head. "I completely forgot about that."

"Well, you better attend or your parents will have a fit."

They continue talking, so I decide to speak with Wren.

"So, what's the plan, exactly?" I inquire.

"Well, now that we've found out that Zayne's the prince, it makes things a lot easier." She gives me a sheepish look. "Originally, my plan was to somehow sneak into the ball, but maybe Zayne will let us in."

"Why do you think the stone will be at the ball?" I ask in confusion.

"The Lochaere is actually quite small. The chance that it's on jewelry is high and people wear jewelry at balls. I can use the locating spell then to narrow it down. The locating spell only works if the stone is close by."

"That's genius, Wren," I say in amazement. I'm even more surprised when I see a slight blush in her cheeks.

"Thanks, Quinn, but it's nothing, really. If anything, it's a bad plan." She shakes her head.

"Maybe not. I wouldn't have thought about the jewelry thing."

She laughs, and it's a beautiful sound. "I think you underestimate your smarts, Quinn."

"Well, if you would have it, I'd be honored to escort you to the ball, madam," I say with a smile as I bow.

Wren plays along. "Oh, it would be my greatest pleasure to be escorted by you, my Lord," she says, giving a goofy curtsy, and I laugh. "I guess now, at least, I don't have to drag someone off the street."

"Oh, trust me, madam. No one *wouldn't* want to escort you to the ball." I wink.

"No, I think you're wrong. I actually have a reputation for scaring people."

"I don't doubt it."

We continue talking about the ball, and it's nice, not worrying about the Sorcerer for some time. Looking at her now, I realize I have to tell her the truth. I can't keep this from her any longer.

"Wren?" I say slowly, and take a deep breath to try to tamp down the panic. This is inevitable. This is the moment I tell her the truth. I know she'll hate me, but I have to tell her. This entire thing has made me realize I care for her.

"Quinn?" she asks, but I can tell she's distracted by something else. I open my mouth, about to speak, but she interrupts me. "Can I ask you something?"

I see her solemn expression and I shut my mouth. Later. I'll tell her later. "Of course."

"Has anyone told you something that made you angry, but as you think about it, you realize they might be right?"

"Sure." I nod, and then pause. "Is this about what happened between Zayne and you?"

She lets out a breath. "Yes. He told me something and I'm afraid I reacted harshly."

"What did he tell you?" I ask hesitantly.

She holds my gaze. Taking a deep breath, she shares what Zayne had said. As she finishes, I stare at my feet in silence. After a moment, I look up, hoping she sees the sincerity in my expression.

Her eyes flood with realization, and she slowly shakes her head. "You agree with him."

"You deserve to be happy."

"You don't understand-"

"Maybe I don't. Maybe I don't because everyone's situation is different. But, Wren, he killed my parents too, and it's taken me a while, but as I spend more time with you and Zayne, I realize that for once in my life, I'm letting myself be happy. And it feels good. I'm tired. I'm tired of stopping myself from laughing and feeling happy." I run my hand through my hair and sigh. "And I want you to experience the same thing. I'm happy Zayne told you, because someone needed to tell you the truth, Wren. He didn't do anything wrong and I think you should talk to him." I hold my breath, hoping she doesn't lash out at me. Instead, immense sadness shows in her eyes.

"I know," she whispers. "But I just can't find it in myself to enjoy life when the thing that killed my parents is still out there." She takes a deep breath. "But I'll try. For you guys, I'll try." She gives me a gentle smile. "Thank you, Quinn."

I give her a bewildered look. "What for?"

"For making me understand."

I shake my head. "You're welcome, but this is all Zayne's doing."

She shuffles her feet. "You're right." She swallows. "I should go apologize."

She gives me a fond smile, and I grin back at her. I'm happy for her.

Before we know it, the castle is looming in front of us in all of its glory. The stone bricks of the palace seem to gleam in the sunlight and green tapestries with the royal family crest hang from the balconies. Flowers grow all around the castle and beautiful vines creep up the stones, reaching for the sun. Many turrets jot up along the walls, and as we approach the gates, one of the guards recognize Lucas and Zayne. Zayne informs them of our status as his guests and they let the drawbridge down.

We walk across the bridge and the watchmen greet Zayne as he passes. Many receive him in the same manner as Lucas, as if they were great friends, and Zayne stops to return their welcome. Once we pass the gates, the castle comes to life. There are many people in the courtyard. Judging by their clothing, they are all nobles or have a great deal of money. I catch a glimpse of the stables and spy attendants running around. People greet each other, and I see servants gathering water from a well.

We enter the castle and are immediately caught in chaos. Servants and maids run around, finishing their errands. I guess this was Lucas' meaning when he said everyone's in a rush because of the upcoming Ball. A maid almost knocks me over, blinded by the amount of fabric, probably for a dress, bundled in her arms. She quickly apologizes, but before I can even react, she's already on the move again.

The castle itself is beautiful. Torches are bolted on the walls, providing warmth and light inside. Many portraits hang on the walls, depicting the royal family and various dukes and other nobles. A sparkling chandelier hangs from the high ceiling and reflects thousands of lights unto the walls. A beautiful staircase climbs up the middle of the gigantic atrium. Lucas excuses himself, saying he should get back to his duties. Zayne stops a young maid and her eyes widen when she realizes it's the prince.

"Your Highness," she says, flustered, as she straightens imaginary wrinkles on her apron and gives a deep bow. She has the look of someone that hasn't been here long.

Zayne shakes his head. "Please, call me Zayne or Nicolaus. And you don't have to bow."

The maid keeps her face blank as she replies, "Of course, Your Highness… Nicolaus."

Zayne gives her a warm smile. "If you don't mind, can you show these two their guest rooms? I have someone I have to meet."

"Of course," she says, still flustered.

"Thank you."

The maid gestures to Wren and I, and then leads us up the staircase. She remains quiet as she takes us farther into the castle.

"It's like a maze in here," Wren whispers to me.

"Hey, at least we'll have an actual bed to sleep in. We haven't had that in forever."

"Thank goodness for that. I'm in much need of a bath."

"I've been worse."

"I'm sure you have."

The maid stops and gestures to two rooms across the hall from each other.

"You can take which ever room you prefer. I'll leave you now so you can get settled." She curtsies and is about to leave, but I stop her.

"If you don't mind me asking, what's your name?"

She seems shocked once more and says, "It's Ann."

"Well, thank you, Ann."

"It's no problem, my Lord."

I shake my head. "Oh, I'm no lord. Please call me Quinn."

She nods and quickly leaves.

Wren smiles. "That was nice of you."

"What?" I ask, confused.

"You asking her name."

I shrug. "It's nothing."

Wren leaves it alone, and I let her take her pick in rooms. She takes the one on the left, and with a wave, shuts the door. I open the door on the right and am stunned by the elaborate décor. I notice that the green and gold theme continues in here as well. There are paintings with gold frames that I bet cost a fortune, and a plush rug lies at the foot of the bed. The bed itself is giant and looks as if it could fit an entire family. Light shines through glass doors leading to the balcony. Beside the wall is a shelf filled with books, thin and wide, and a drawer is shoved against the wall.

I step inside gradually and my eyes widen when I realize there is an adjoining room to the bedroom. It appears to be a small common area, with a table, more books, and even a fireplace. A chair is in a corner, facing the window that gives a view of the gardens below. It's like I'm in a dream. Working for Damien gave me a lot of money, but nothing compares to this. If Damien found out that I had access to the inside of the castle of Elrea, who knows what he would do?

He's not going to find out. He would take full advantage and try to gain more power.

The bed calls out to me, and the second I lay my head on the soft pillows, exhaustion overcomes me.

CHAPTER 33

WREN

I LIE IN BED, shocked. I can't believe that he's the prince. I try to find an ounce of anger that he hid this from us, but I can't. We haven't known each other for long and everyone has their secrets. By the end of this journey, if we are all still alive, we will all probably go our separate ways anyhow.

I wake up later and squint at the light seeping in through the window. I didn't even know that I fell asleep, but my body feels better with more energy. The bed probably helps. I get up and, as I'm rubbing my eyes, I hear a hollow knock on the door.

"Come in," I say, out of habit.

The door opens, and a woman enters with a servant following behind, carrying a tub.

"I'm Lorelle. If you need anything, I'm here. I'm your maid while you remain a guest of the palace."

I shake my head. "No, I don't need a maid."

She looks at me sternly and replies, "This is not a request. A guest of the palace will be treated like a guest."

I shut my mouth and just nod. I don't know what else to say.

"Now," she continues, "you need to take a bath. From what Zayne told me, you have been on the road for quite a while."

Again, I can tell that it isn't a request, but I don't mind. For once, it feels good to be pampered.

The servant steps up and, moments later, more servants walk in with hot water, pouring it into the tub. "Would you like me to help you, my Lady?" Lorelle asks me.

"No, I'll be okay. And I'm no lady."

Lorelle shakes her head. "The way I see it, anyone who is a friend of the prince is a lady to me."

As if on cue, there's a knock on the door and Zayne's voice filters through. "Wren?"

Lorelle grumbles. "He can't even wait until you take a bath."

I laugh. "It's fine, Lorelle."

She raises an eyebrow. "Not if you're smelling what I'm smelling right now."

I roll my eyes. "Come in!"

Zayne slips inside and Lorelle says, "That's my cue to leave." As she disappears past him, Zayne hovers under the doorway with an uncomfortable look on his face, probably remembering our argument.

"How is the room, is everything okay?" he asks, hesitantly, and looks at me with caution, as if I'm going to lash out.

I smile. "Everything is perfect."

He pauses and then nods. "Good."

He makes a move to leave, but I call out, "Wait."

He turns with a look of confusion.

"I'm sorry," I rush out in one breath.

Realization makes its way into his expression. "For?" he asks steadily. He knows, but he wants me to say it.

I deserve this, but still groan inside. "For treating you like I did, when you were just telling the truth. It was wrong and I'm sorry. I understand if you're mad at me."

His eyes soften and he smiles. "I was never mad at you." As if realizing something, he squints at me. "You called what I said the truth."

Gulping, I take a step closer to him. "You were right. About everything. What Quinn and you said has made me realize that."

"What did Quinn say?" he asks in confusion.

I shrug. "That you are right and that he knows what it feels like to be so clouded with the intent of revenge."

He shakes his head. "You know, at first, I thought we couldn't trust him. But he's proving me wrong. He's not that bad."

I smile, remembering how he asked me to the ball. "Yeah."

"I'm happy for you, Wren. That you're giving yourself the chance to live life to the fullest." With that, he turns and leaves the room.

A warm feeling rushes through me, and I realize that it's nice to have people who care about you. Who just want the best for you. Zayne is turning into the brother that I've never had, and I find that I don't mind.

CHAPTER 34

ZAYNE

I WALK WITH INTENT, thinking about my conversation with Wren. I really am happy for her. I only want the best for her; she's like a sister to me.

I finally arrive at the ballroom doors and push them open. Before this, I had quickly stopped by my room to clean up. Who knows what Mother would do if she found me in my dirt-caked clothes? I step into the ballroom, which is nearly unrecognizable because of all the decorations. It's the most chaotic area in the castle right now, and in the middle of it all is my mother. She tells one of the maids to shift the decorations of leaves hanging on the wall a little more to the left. No flowers for the Autumn Ball.

"No, no. Now it's too far to the left," she says in frustration.

"Mother, leave the poor girl alone," I say, laughing.

Mother's eyes go wide as she swivels around in surprise. "Zayne?" she says, shocked. Then, she appears to remember that she is the queen and quickly composes herself. "I didn't know you were coming back so soon." She maintains her poise, but the light stays in her eyes.

I walk up and kiss her on the cheek. "Oh, Mother. If you wanted me to be gone so bad, you should have told me."

She smiles. "I missed your witty banter. Do Sebastian and Rose know you are back yet?"

I shake my head. "You're the first person. Well, you and the maids. Word travels fast; they'll find out soon enough."

As if on cue, I hear a familiar voice behind me. "Brother?"

I turn around and grin to see Sebastian.

He jogs across the room, his strawberry blond hair in familiar disarray. "Why didn't you tell me you were here?"

"Surprise?" I say sheepishly.

He narrows his eyes. "Hilarious."

"Alright, alright. I'm sorry."

He frowns for a good, solid minute with me awkwardly fidgeting before him, and then he breaks into a smile and hugs me. "I've missed you."

"I've missed you too."

He pulls away and pats me on the shoulder. "We have a lot of catching up to do. Does Rose know you're here yet?"

I shake my head. "No, but I'm planning to go search for her now. Do you know where she is?"

He gives me a look. "Where do you think?" Ah, right.

I turn to leave, but he stops me with a hand on my shoulder. "Come find me later, alright?"

I nod and he lets me go. I walk out of the chaotic ballroom and head down the hallway. I continue past the portraits and great atrium, as Mother likes to call it. Finally, I reach the massive oak doors with golden handles. A guard stands out in front and he bows upon seeing me. "Your Highness."

William is my sister's bodyguard, has been since she was born. He's a nice man in his forties, and even though I insist on his not referring to me with such formality, he doesn't listen.

I smile at him. "William."

His face, as usual, doesn't show any emotion, so I can't tell if he's surprised to see that I'm back. I push on the golden handles and slowly enter the library, the grand doors shutting carefully behind me. Opinions could vary on the palace, but our library is doubtlessly one of the best.

It is a giant, circular room with shelves that surround visitors, reaching all the way to the ceiling, separated into three floors with access to all the books. Another shelf circles the one in the middle, with the same three-floored layout and four rectangular holes on each floor to access the second shelf. Similarly, there is a third and a fourth shelf, the fourth being the largest and encompassing all the others. Elegant, spiraling black staircases connect each floor, and inside the first shelf, at the very center of the room, is a common area with couches and tables that allow visitors to sit down and read. There isn't a fireplace, for fear that the library will burn down. Luckily, it isn't winter right now, but the cold never stops Rose, despite Mother telling her she'll get sick.

I look around and don't see Rose in the common room, but I wasn't expecting her to be – she almost never is. I ascend the staircases to reach the top floor, enjoying the smell of the books. I eventually arrive at the highest level and, after walking through the shelves, finally reach the outermost one. There, sitting on her favorite window seat, is Rose with a book in her hands. She stares intently into the pages, as lost in words as usual.

She doesn't notice me right away. Her pale pink gown compliments her strawberry-blonde hair, and she looks peaceful and content sitting there. I suddenly have an urge not to disturb her, and am about to turn around and leave when she suddenly looks up, as if she sensed my presence. When her brown eyes land on mine, her jaw drops in shock.

"Nico?" She springs up and crashes into me with a force many would be surprised to discover. Her arms encircle my waist, and she holds on to me tightly. "I missed you," she mumbles against my clothes.

"I missed you even more."

I love my siblings more than anything. She won't let go, so after a few minutes, I gently pry her off. "I got you something."

Her eyes widen and she tucks a strand of hair behind her ear. "Really? What is it?" she says excitingly.

I reach into the satchel still hanging from my shoulder and take out the tiny wooden hummingbird I bought in a small town. It's blue and has intricate details I knew she would like.

"It's for me?" she says in awe.

I nod, and she gasps and snatches it from my hand. Anything I give, she finds fascinating. She's seven, so I shouldn't expect anything else. I devote another hour to Rose in the library, talking about what books she's read, and find myself missing the time I used to spend with her, not worrying about my duty as a prince or about saving the world. Here, I'm just her brother.

However, the moment quickly fades when I hear footsteps. William approaches, and he gives a slight bow. "Your father has summoned you, Your Highness."

I flinch inside, but nod. "Thank you, William." I was hoping to put this off for later. I give my farewell to Rose and exit the library.

When I enter my father's study, his back is to the fire-place, and I find myself hesitating to let myself be known. I can just turn and walk away, but I know that will make the situation worse, so I knock on the open wooden door with the back of my hand. My father turns and I imme-diately regret coming. His brown eyes are currently filled with anger.

"Take a seat, Nicholaus," he says, showing no emotion on his face.

"I'm fine standing," I reply and he gives me a harsh look.

His stare remains for a couple of seconds. "I said take a seat."

I can hear the barely concealed anger and sit down before I make anything worse. He continues gazing at the fireplace for a long time, and I shove down annoyance. Everything is always on his time.

When he finally looks up, I can see the full extent of his anger and stop myself from flinching. Funny how I've gone through so much in my life, but one look can make me feel vulnerable. One would imagine this much anger was too great for just showing up earlier than I said I would, and that assessment wouldn't be wrong, but deep down I know it is more than that.

After I became the captain of the guard, my father didn't act like my father. A prince becoming a captain of the guard was unheard of, even though I didn't actually guard. Instead, I went on missions with the Gavreel Society and took care of matters that seemed of threat to the kingdom in anyway. Other than that, I trained our future captain of the guards in certain forms of combat, but now my second in command takes care of the rest of their training.

When I became captain of the guard, I ensured that I made no mistakes, so my father couldn't find an excuse to lash out at me. This instead gave him an opportunity to voice what he felt about me – all the disappointment that I didn't turn out like my older brother, a man who was concerned with politics and such. My brother isn't a bad person; however, he didn't mingle with the common people as much as I did, and my father hates that I do because he thinks that 'I shouldn't stoop to their level.'

My father eventually speaks. "How dare you embarrass your family like that? Do you understand how it looks when the prince of Elrea is revealed at a baker's stand after looking like he was hiding from someone? You have lost your sense of duty. You should be in the palace, putting your classes of politics to use and actually helping this kingdom grow."

I repress the anger I feel and, in a controlled voice, say, "I am helping the kingdom. You know those deaths are a huge problem. There's something out there and I have to stop it from doing more harm. The Gavree-"

My father cuts me off, "Again, with your silly society, acting like you're doing something useful."

"But I am! In fact, I'm headed to stop the problem once and for all."

This piques my father's interest and he stands taller. "And how is that?"

I open my mouth to tell him about the Sorcerer, but I shut it just as quickly. He would never believe me

He scowls. "That's what I thought. You won't be leaving again. After the Autumn Ball, your post as the captain of the guard will be no longer."

I freeze. "*What?* You can't do that. You have no right!"

"*I have all the right!* How dare you argue with me?" he shouts.

I open my mouth once again to shout back, but I close it a second time. I silently walk out of the room, not caring for the consequences of not asking the king for permission to leave.

Once I am away from his eyes, I hunch over. I should go back in there and fight, but I don't. I'm a coward.

I grit my teeth, straighten my back, and rush toward my room to change into more comfortable clothing.

Before I know it, I'm headed to the specialized training arena in the castle. As I approach, I hear the familiar sounds of weapons clashing and people shouting combat orders, and it automatically comforts me. This is what I grew up with. I open the door and walk in. A few people are doing hand-to-hand combat on the mats, while others work on weapons. There's a small group of new faces next to the weapons shelf, and I see Lucas instructing them on each weapon and how to use them. New recruits.

"Zayne!" a voice says and I see my second-in-command, Raulin. Raulin is a few years older than me, but we started our training together. He is a stern, serious man. "Where have you been?"

"Out there, saving the world from destruction," I say, only half joking, but Raulin laughs.

"Fair enough."

I nod toward an empty mat. "Spar with me?"

We walk toward the mat and take our positions across from each other. Our ready forms move in a wide circle as we look for an opening, and when Raulin lunges with a fist, I duck before sweeping my leg to knock him off balance, but he sees it and jumps before we start circling again. Soon, I get lost in the familiar motions and welcome the pain that comes when Raulin hits me. I counter the move and hit him back. Before I know it, my muscles are sore and Raulin gives a motion that he needs a break. I wipe the sweat off my forehead with my arm and breathe deeply.

The doors suddenly open then, and I jolt in surprise to see that it's Wren. What is she doing here? She looks around in discomfort and I follow her gaze. Everyone has stopped what they were doing and now all look at her with curiosity. A female has never stepped in here before. Wren's eyes then land on me, and she hesitantly waves. Everyone follows her gaze and look between us.

I walk up to her and, gazing down in puzzlement, ask her, "What are you doing here?"

She looks up at me and carefully says, "What everyone else is doing. Do you mind if I use the weapons?" I can tell she is still cautious toward me because of what I said at the gypsy camp, but at least she doesn't look angry any longer. I nod and she grins.

"Good." She heads to the other side of the room, fixated on the targets while ignoring all the stares, and picks up some daggers.

"Sure you know how to use those?" one of the soldiers asks, jokingly. Oh no, he's going to regret saying that.

Wren ignores him, takes her stance in front of a target, and, without hesitating, throws the dagger. Everyone in the room watches with bated breath as the knife appears to fly in slow motion before sinking into the bulls-eye. A collective gasp travels through the room and I grin.

"Lucky shot," the same man says, but now he appears less certain.

Once again, Wren doesn't reply, but resets her stance before unleashing the second dagger, which hits the bulls-eye spot-on. Someone lets out a low whistle, and Wren looks at the soldier, one eyebrow raised. He lifts both of his hands in surrender and chuckles.

"Okay, back to before," I say loudly and everyone

appears to break out of a spell, continuing like nothing happened. I shake my head and walk up to Wren. "Show-off."

"Hey! I had to show him not to underestimate a woman."

"Fair enough. I think you succeeded."

Wren moves on to the bow and arrow, and while she doesn't hit the bulls-eye each time, she strikes the closest inner circle. Everyone training nearby acts like they don't notice, but I can tell they are watching her from the corner of their eyes. I chuckle when I remember their shocked faces.

My mood has officially been lifted.

CHAPTER 35

QUINN

TONIGHT, WREN AND I are invited to eat with the royal family, but, really, it isn't a request. Saying no to a royal family is out of the question. Yet, the entire thing feels like a dream. The Black Assassin eating with the royal family, and not because of a mission. I take a walk around the castle, expecting someone to stop me, but no one does. I watch the people getting ready for the Autumn Ball and I think about how I asked Wren if I could take her. An unfamiliar feeling stirs inside me and I gasp when I realize that it's excitement. I am excited to go to a ball of all things.

I enter my room with this new revelation to see an expensive red tunic and a pair of trousers lying on my bed. Luckily, I hid all my stuff in case someone came into the room, but it's still unsettling to know others were in here without my knowledge. This must be what they expect me to wear for the dinner. I frown. They probably think

I don't have any clothes fit enough for the royal family, and while I do have a lot, I left them behind; they weren't practical for the trip.

Once I put on the clothes, I walk across the hallway and knock on Wren's door. She opens it a little and peeks into the hallway. "Quinn?" she asks with surprise.

"Hey, I was wondering if you wanted to walk with me to dinner. If you're ready?"

"I would love to. I was just about to leave anyway."

She opens the door a little more and then steps into the hallway. She's replaced her shirt and pants for a gray gown that brings out her eyes. I offer her my arm, and we both walk to the dining room together. We talk about useless things, nothing to do with the Sorcerer and the mission. It's nice. She talks about how she used to live in the city until her parents died. I talk about my little sister and how she's the only family I had left, how I'll do anything to keep her safe. I know this is the perfect time to confess to her who I really am, but I can't bring myself to do that. I can't ruin this moment.

"Sometimes, I wonder how things would be if magic didn't exist," Wren says quietly, after a moment of silence.

My breath stalls. "Why?"

She lets out a soft sigh. "Things would be a whole lot less complicated."

I pull her closer. Can't argue with that. If magic didn't exist, my parents would have never died; I never would have become the monster I am now; I could never have met Wren and actually have a chance with her. Wren would have parents, and a whole lot of lives would have been saved. The list goes on and on.

Finally, I say, "Life is full of 'what ifs,' but we can't change anything. We have to take the choices life throws at us and make them into something worth living for."

I'm such a hypocrite.

Wren falls silent after that and we soon enter the dining room. Stepping in, I look around. The room is spacious, with a chandelier hanging in the middle. A long table stretches through the center of the room, but there are only plates on one side of it. The walls are golden and the ceiling is a mirror, reflecting our faces back at us. I notice that the only person to have arrived, as of yet, is Zayne. He stands when we enter, and I realize this is the first time we've had a chance to talk since discovering he's a prince.

He looks at us, and then, as if it were unbearable, gazes at his feet before diverting his sight to the wall behind us. Finally, his eyes settle on ours, and I spy sincerity there. "I am so sorry I didn't tell you guys sooner. Words cannot express how sorry I am, but I had no choice. Being the prince puts me in danger at all times."

There's a moment of silence, and it appears that he's holding his breath, waiting for one of us to speak.

I finally do. "I understand. There are always reasons for secrets, and I understand why you kept this one. As you said, we are friends. Friends are there for each other."

I think about my own secret and how little his is compared to mine. When they find out, they won't be as forgiving. And they will find out, because I have to tell them sooner or later. When I don't complete this mission, Damien will send assassins after me. Despite that, the only thing that's prevented me from leaving without looking back is my sister.

Wren smiles. "We're not mad, and like Quinn said, we understand."

Zayne grins in relief. He guides us to our chairs, and we sit and talk for a while. After waiting a couple of minutes, the doors open with a flourish and the royal family enters. We immediately stand up. First come the king and the queen. The king's stern and calculating eyes are a sharp contrast to the queen's welcoming ones, yet there's something about her that tells me she's not to be messed with. The king gives us a short glance and then looks dismissively away, but the queen graces us with a smile.

I guess that's the only introduction we're going to get. Prince Sebastian walks in with the little princess, Rose. They are a sharp contrast to their parents. Sebastian's face is open, with an easy grin. He automatically seems like a man who you can trust; an important trait in a future king. Rose scurries next to him, hurrying to keep up with her brother's long strides. She looks at us shyly and Wren smiles at her, a gesture which she returns with a tentative smile of her own. Immediately, after we are all seated, people wearing matching uniforms come from a side door, holding platters.

As they set food on the table, Sebastian leans toward us like he's sharing a secret. "So how much did my brother pay you?"

Wren tilts her head in confusion. "What?"

"To act like you're his friends." He then grins to show he's joking.

Zayne rolls his eyes, but there is a smile on his face. "You're one to talk. I would be surprised to see you interacting with anyone."

Sebastian laughs, but it cut off when the king speaks with concealed anger. "Don't speak to your future king that way."

Sebastian's smile fades away, and Zayne looks down at his plate. "He was joking, Father. If it is anyone's fault, it is mine. I started it."

It seems like everyone is holding their breath to see what happens next, but the king just remains silent. He stays like that the entire dinner, while Sebastian asks us questions about how we met Zayne. We had already come up with a cover story for just such an eventuality. We stick as close to the truth as possible, and explain that Zayne and Wren met at an inn where she was waitressing, and I met the pair of them at a library.

Luckily, everyone bought it, but the king didn't even seem to care about the whole ordeal. Some type of king he is. They should improve the security around this place, and I remind myself to tell Zayne later. Despite the change of mood in this dinner, the food was some of the best I've ever tried. There is a huge variety, originating from as far as Junskart, up north. Their cooks really did a good job.

From the corner of my eye, I spy movement and turn to see Wren hiding away a spoon in her sleeve. She freezes upon realizing I've caught her, and I raise an eyebrow. She shifts uncomfortably in her seat and avoids my gaze, but then looks back at me before glancing away once more, as if facing me is so dreary to her. I restrain a building laugh, all the while imagining why she just stole silverware from the table.

The rest of dinner is uneventful and, before I know it, I'm back in my room. I reach into the satchel I had hidden within a crevice between the bed and the wall earlier, and drink another vial of the flower mixture. There is a faint scent of garbage to the potion, I notice with disgust as it slides down my throat. Maybe this is a hint of what Zayne and Wren smelled when the potion was first made. I don't even want to think about that odor.

Time passes quickly, and before I know it, it is the day before the Autumn Celebration Ball. People are even more frantic than usual and hurry to resolve any last-minute preparations. By this point, there are even more guests in the palace, and many are calling up maids and servants to help them with something or the other. Tired of sitting idle, I decide to knock on Wren's door and ask if she's up for a walk. She agrees, and we start trekking toward the garden.

"So…" I look at her. "What are you wearing for the ball? I'm pretty sure you didn't pack a gown in your satchel."

She laughs and rubs the back of her neck. "Yeah, Lorelle told me that she's making a dress herself, and it will be ready by tonight. It was very kind of her."

I smile. "That's amazing, Wren."

She looks at me. "What about you?"

I smile. "One of the servants came up to my room and told me that he'll have clothing ready by tonight as well." I frown. "I'm not even going to ask how he knows my measurements. I'm pretty sure he's the one who provided the outfit for the dinner as well."

Wren chuckles. "Maybe he has a good eye? I knew this woman in my village who was like that."

We continue walking before I halt suddenly. "Wren?"

She looks back at me and frowns. "What's the matter?"

"If you don't have magic, how will you cast your summoning spell to find the other half of the Lochaere?"

She relaxes. "One step ahead of you. Remember when I did a spell inside the town created by the Sorcerer without using my magic?" I nod and she continues, "So, I'll be doing the same thing and use objects that I have with me to create the spell."

"Do you have everything you need for tonight?"

She gives a sheepish smile. "Not really," she says hesitantly. "I need something else. But don't worry, I'll find what I need before the ball."

Despite her confidence, I hear a note of fear and immediately know there's more that she's not telling me.

"What is it exactly?"

She gulps and looks at the ground. "Fairy wings."

I choke. "What?" We hear a rustle of leaves and both freeze.

A white cat scurries across the pathway before disappearing in the hedges. I sigh in relief and again focus on Wren.

"Fairy wings," she repeats in a whisper.

I immediately think about the engravings of the fairies on Damien's door. I frown. "How are you going to get fairy wings?" I know I should be freaking out about the fact that there are fairies, but there's magic and witches, so why not?

She looks up, but avoids meeting my gaze. "Don't worry about it."

I open my mouth to argue, but she looks at me then with a stern look in her eyes. She isn't going to budge, so I decide to drop it. Against my will, I feel sudden dread. There's a reason she's not telling me, and I don't even want to think about what that can mean. But I know that Wren is a stubborn person and she won't confess to me.

We continue walking in the garden, and Wren speaks up. "You know, they say there have been tons of people who went missing in this garden."

I glance at her. "What?"

She nods. "Yeah. Apparently, people tend to avoid this place now."

I look at her, bewildered. "Then what are we doing here?"

"I want to find out why," she says with a determined look on her face. "It can't be a coincidence."

"One of these days, you're going to get yourself killed."

She rolls her eyes. "Come on. Apparently, all the disappearances happened on the west side."

I let out a sigh of resignation and let her drag me by the arm; her gray eyes are filled with curiosity and excitement. The farther we walk, the more unkempt everything becomes. The bushes and plants show that no one has trimmed them, and weeds flourish under our feet. No one has come here in a long, long time, I think as we pass a broken fountain run dry. The stone pathway is cracked and my guard immediately goes up. I felt an alien, intruding force in the air and I frown.

"Maybe we shouldn't do this," I say as I look back to Wren, but feel panic when I don't see her. Dread sets in and I swallow hard. "Wren? Wren?" Where is she? I look around in panic and am about to turn back when a scream cuts through the air. "Wren!"

I run toward the voice, but the only things surrounding me are the tall hedges. I clench my hands and look around as I feel sweat starting to form on my brow line. I hear a sudden growl and I turn to the hedges, confused. It seemed like the noise had come from inside them. Curiously, I shove my hand into the hedge and push forward until the leaves are at my elbow, before pulling back immediately. My breathing escalates.

There is only air on the other side. Before I can second-guess what I'm about to do, I run into the hedges with my eyes closed. Slowly the feeling of leaves is replaced with air; I hear another scream and whip my eyes open to take in the scene before me. Wren sits up from where she is on the ground and looks in front of her with fear in her eyes. With a sick feeling in my stomach, I follow her gaze and stagger back when I see a white creature. The creature itself is covered in white scales and resembles a dragon, except its head is more like a snake. Its bloodshot red eyes stare blankly at Wren. It hisses and reveals black, deadly teeth.

It approaches Wren, and it is about to lunge at her when I shout, "Hey!"

Immediately, its attention latches on to me and it hisses before making a run in my direction. I dive out of the way at the last moment and look at Wren, who is now standing.

"What is that?" I shout at her.

"I- I think this is in one of the stories in my mom's book. It's called a Zarjuk!"

Zarjuk? "Well, does it have a weak spot?" I ask her as I lunge out of its way once again.

"It's the base of the throat."

All right, at least it has one. "Okay, here's the plan. You distract it, and I'll try to kill it." Wren looks at me, her face pale. "Wren?"

She finally nods and takes a dagger out of her boot. She pulls her arm back, lets the dagger fly, and it harmlessly bounces off the monster; however, it is enough for the attention to shift from me to her.

The Zarjuk cocks its head at her and blinks before letting out another hiss. It slowly makes its way toward her like she's prey, and I feel sick. I can't miss my shot. Not now. Before it lunges at her, I run at it from the side and slide on my knees, snatching up Wren's fallen dagger as I go. I raise my arm and use the dagger to slit its throat. The creature screams as a black shimmer surrounds it. I blink my eyes, and in front of me is the white kitten from before. This time it is still, and I know it's dead.

"What in the world?" I whisper.

Wren glances at me before looking back at the cat.

"Zarjuks have the power to shape shift into one creature. In this instance, it is a cat. Zarjuks aren't the brightest creatures, though."

I run a shaking hand through my hair and look at Wren. "Are you alright?"

She nods, but shudders. "One second I was behind you, and the next, I felt something grab me and we are here." She pauses and looks around. "Where are we, anyway?"

I let out a laugh. "You're not going to believe this. We're inside the hedges."

She scrunches up her nose. "That doesn't make any sense."

"See for yourself," I tell her before walking back out of the hedge. I wait on the other side for a few moments, before Wren's hand makes its appearance through the foliage. Her whole body follows right after.

She has a look of awe on her face as she stares at the hedge. "It's unbelievable. Most likely, no one knows it exists. That was probably why so many people went missing."

I'm about to comment until I see her shoulders. Noticing that I have fallen silent, she turns to look at me, but I keep my eyes on her shoulders. She frowns and asks, "Quinn?"

I reach out to touch her shoulder and the crimson blood there is in sharp contrast to my skin, still ashen from what just happened. Wren looks at my hand in shock before turning her head to see the wounds. There are four gashes that run deep, and blood stains her shirt.

"I di- didn't even realize," Wren stutters out. "It must have happened when it grabbed me."

I press my lips together tightly and put my hand on her back. "Come on, let's take you to the infirmary."

I shift my weight to begin walking, but she digs her heals into the ground. "They'll ask questions."

"No, they won't." She gives me a look of doubt and I sigh. "Trust me. They don't do that at royal infirmaries. The nurses wouldn't risk talking about it or questioning anything. The royals like to keep matters a secret."

She reluctantly follows me after that, and we head inside to the infirmary.

I look at her. "Are you ever going to tell me why you stole that spoon?"

"No."

ZAYNE

I am in my room when the messenger comes knocking on my door. Without a word, he hands me a letter and leaves. I peer down the hall and stare at his receding back in confusion.

I look at the letter in my hands as I close the door and flip it over. The insignia of the Gavreel Society seals the envelope and I rip it open, holding my breath. I immediately recognize the handwriting. Archer. I quickly start reading the letter and the more I read, the more my frown deepens.

More deaths, and they were close to Elrea this time. I crumble up the letter and toss it into the fire. I rub my eyes in frustration. We have to hurry and we have little time left.

CHAPTER 36

WREN

I JUST *HAVE* TO lose my powers, I think as I angrily trudge through the dark forest surrounding the kingdom. The shadows jump at me as the crickets make their sound. If I had told Zayne or Quinn where I was going, they both would have told me it was too dangerous. They would have stopped me from going or they would have come with me. And I can't let them do that. It's too dangerous.

When I told Quinn that it wasn't a big deal to get fairy wings, that was a lie. A terrible lie. To get fairy wings, it's necessary to journey through the forest at midnight during the full moon, and the fairies will find those who seek them.

Tonight, there's a full moon, and I am trying to stumble into a fairy circle. Sure, this may seem wonderful if fairies were really the kind, beautiful things most people read about in bedtime stories. They're not. Instead, these are the ones found in dark books that hold more truth than readers imagine. And here I am, purposely trying to stumble on one like a fool.

However, I guess I have a mild advantage. Because I am a daughter of magic, it is slightly harder for me to fall victim to the fairies' curse, but I'm still in danger of being enveloped in one if I'm within their circle for too long. Plus, what I'm searching for will make them hate me even more.

No fairy would voluntarily give their wings, but they love games and have great pride. I have to make a deal with them. My mother told me stories about making contracts with the fairies. They have to keep their word and are magically bound to maintaining their part of the deal. So, as she explained, the first step is making the fairy actually say the words, 'It's a deal.' However, when making a contract with a fairy, the same rules apply to the second party. I must also say those words - the fairies will make sure of it - and I am also bound by magic to uphold my end of the deal.

The night grows darker until I can't see my hand in front of me. I lose track of time and begin to feel doubt creep into my mind. What am I doing?

My eyes are starting to blur when I hear a muted sound. I pause and shake my head, thinking I am imagining things, but then I hear it again. I stumble toward the source, and the noise starts to take shape into music. Soon, a flickering orange light comes into my vision and grows closer as I approach it. Glassy laughter and shouts join the taunting beats of a drum, and I feel an odd urge to dance. By now, I am fully awake and realize that this must be the fairy circle. I slow down and cautiously make my way to the trees and peer around cautiously. A small gasp escapes past my lips as I take note of the scene before me.

Fairies of various colors dance in a drunken trance as others play the drums. A fire is in the middle of the circle and their dagger-like teeth glint in the light. I swallow hard and take a step back.

"What do we have here?" a haughty voice says from behind me. The voice is like glass, but there is a bite to it, only just concealed. I swivel around and in front of me is a gray fairy with black, wispy hair. Her eyes are like a black abyss, and her face is painted with a look of disdain.

Pure fear rushes through me, and when she steps forward, I step back with wide eyes. Suddenly I remember something and reach into my pocket, retrieving the spoon I snatched from the dinner. The handle of the spoon is made of iron, and even though that seems unusual, noble people are constantly trying to outclass their fellow peers, even when it came to a spoon.

Thankfully, Quinn was the only one who noticed that I hid it up my sleeve. When I pull the spoon out, the fairy hisses as she senses the iron, but then she smirks. "Silly human. That can't help you. That's not enough." Iron is deadly to fairies, but only in large quantities. If the spoon touched her, though, it would definitely burn her and leave a scar, but I know it can't protect me from all of them.

"Stay away from me." I'm surprised at how strong my

voice is and I brandish my spoon in front of me like a sword.

She gives out a laugh of broken glass and glances at something behind me. "It's not me you have to worry about."

I endeavor not to tremble as I look over my shoulder. Without knowing it, I have backed up slightly into the circle. There is a pause as the fairies stare at me. And it isn't a curious stare – no, it is a fixation that one has upon finding a new toy to play with, and it makes me recoil. The silence left as soon as it had come, however, and at once, the fairies start nipping at my hair and skin.

I cover my face with my hands as they pull me. I feel cuts on my legs as they tear my trousers. Just when I think I can't handle anymore, a sharp whistle cuts through the air and all the fairies let go. I wince as I gingerly feel the cuts on my face. The music has stopped, and when I open my eyes, there is a fairy, the average height of my hand, with a balding head of oily green hair that reminds me of seaweed. His small eyes appear to sink into his transparent blue face, and his lips are parted to make way for his dagger-like teeth. He tilts his head up and sniffs. Something flashes in his black eyes as his face whips to me.

"You're not human." He smiles. "Looks like we have an Arobol on our hands," he says, referring to the descendants of magic welders.

A murmur ripples through the crowd, and the fairy seems to revel in the attention.

"I'm here to strike a deal," I say, and a collective gasp travels through the crowd.

"What exactly do you want?" The fairy asks, suspicion lacing his voice.

"Right after I win, I want a set of fairy wings and to safely leave the forest without harm, taking the wings with me. No dark creature can follow me out of the forest." I see the look of disbelief on their faces, and a couple of fairies snarl at me. I look at the one in charge and I see hesitation. "Unless you're afraid, of course."

The fairy makes a harsh frown before providing another sickly grin. "Okay."

I can tell that he understood my detailed explanation. Fairies always try to find back-ways and loopholes. If I only asked for the fairy wings, they would make a move to get them back from me, maybe even with lethal force.

"Say the words."

"What words?" he asks, acting naive.

I grit my teeth and give him a hard stare, unmoving.

His grin disappears and he sneers. "You know your stuff, girly. Fine, but I must get something when you lose, and you will lose."

I tilt my head, trying not to show him my worry. "What exactly do you want?"

He scans me from head to toe and smiles. "I want your necklace."

My breath catches. "What?"

"I want your necklace."

"There has to be something else," I start, but the fairy shakes his head. I frown. "Okay."

"Then it's a deal," he says, sealing it.

"It's a deal," I reluctantly add. "What's the game?"

"A riddle. You answer correctly then you win. If not, then I win." I nod in agreement, and he continues, "I have seen water farther than the eyes can see, yet have crossed it with ease. How so?"

I try to tune out the excited chatter of the fairies and think. Crossed it with ease. I glare at the grass trying to think.

"Tick tock, girly," he sneers.

I blurt out the answer, hoping it's right. "It was dew. You walked through dew," I say. I look up to see anger flash across his eyes.

"That's right." He sighs.

A clamor rises, and the fairies step forward, angry, but before they can do anything, the fairy who had just lost raises his hand.

"We must honor the deal. No harm comes to her."

The fairies back up slowly while he steps up. In his hands are fairy wings that had not been there seconds before. "These are the wings I shed when I was a child to make way for the ones that I have now. Use them well," he says, solemn.

I nod and back out of the circle, aware of their eyes on me. When they finally disappear from view, I turn and run, eager to get as far from the fairies as I can. Reaching the palace, I slow down to avoid any suspicion and make my way into my room.

When I enter, I'm startled to find a gorgeous gown lies on the bed. It's strapless and a shimmering, glittering gold color that slowly bleeds to a vibrant red. Shocked, I hesitantly reach out my arm and touch the soft material. Silk. I could feed an entire village with this dress.

I quickly take out the fairy wings and crush them into a mixture for the location spell. The concoction turns a deep purple and I carefully dip my fragment of the Lochaere into it before placing the necklace back around my throat. After I finish, I hesitantly dress myself in the gown and try not to get lost in all the fabric. I finally look in the mirror. Shocked, I take a step back. It's like the dress was made for me. The gown causes my hips to look smaller than they are and the fabric slightly drifts across my legs. It goes all the way to my toes, and some even trails on the floor. I look like the fairies my mom would tell stories about.

I hear a knock on the door before Lorelle walks in. When she sees me in the dress, she appears surprised. Her eyes turn gentle. "You look beautiful. You remind me of my daughter."

I frown. "I wish you could come as well."

She gives a soft laugh. "No, darling. Dancing isn't really my thing." She remembers something. "Did you wear the corset?"

I shake my head firmly. "No. No. I am not wearing a corset. I'm already wearing a gown."

Lorelle sighs. "Well, I can't force you. Can I?" I shake my head and she laughs. "I should have figured. Anyhow, I don't think this dress will look good with the typical rounded shape toward the bottom. No matter what, you are letting me do your hair and face."

I'm about to protest, but she gives a 'don't mess with

me' look and I close my mouth. She leads me to the dresser and instructs me to sit down on the cushioned seat. I take my place and immediately feel awkward. I've never been pampered like this.

"You have a pretty face, so don't worry. I'm not going to cover it up. Just accent what you already have."

She takes a brush off the table and starts gently combing through my hair. The feeling breeds comfort and I close my eyes. The act reminds me of when my mother would do this every morning, whenever she was home. Tears fill my eyes and I quickly blink them away.

I must have a bitter look on my face, because Lorelle asks me, "Are you okay, dear?"

I nod and smile. All I can hope for is that my parents are proud of who I am today. Lorelle puts down the brush and immediately gets to work on my hair.

"Do you have any family, Lorelle?" I ask to pass the time.

I see her smile in the mirror. "Yes, I have a son and a daughter. My daughter is the older one at eleven, and my son is five. Blessed with an angel's smile, both of them. Do you have any siblings?"

"No, but sometimes I wish I did. The company would be nice." But I resist telling her that I'm also glad I don't, because I don't want them to suffer like I have and live their lives only wanting revenge. To be honest, the Ball is a nice reprieve.

"I understand. I'm an only-child myself," she says. "Father wasn't too happy about that. He wanted a son like everyone else." She says this lightly, but I hear the sadness in her voice.

She eventually finishes my hair and then moves on to my face. Taking up the powder, she lightly dabs it on my skin before putting who-knows-what on my features. After what seems forever, she says, "Okay, I'm done."

She moves away so I can see myself in the reflection and I'm shocked at the face staring back at me. My brown hair is tied into a loose bun at the nape of my neck with a curl of hair let loose that tickles my cheek. Multiple braids are woven in with gold ribbons as well, giving off a regal look. Lorelle was right; she didn't cover up my face, but instead accented it. My gray eyes stand out more than ever because of the black kohl surrounding them, making them look stormy. My lips are tinted red, and a soft blush lies on my cheeks. Small white diamonds hang from my ears.

I- I look like my mother. And definitely not like a peasant.

"You look beautiful. You're going to be the object of envy at the Ball," she says sweetly. She taps a finger on her chin. "What are you missing?" Her eyes light up. "Shoes and gloves."

She goes into the closet in search of the footwear, and when she's not looking, I quickly slip a dagger into my holster under the dress. Just in case. You never know. She comes back with a pair of shoes and motions for me to sit on the bed. She hands me the gloves and I slip them on.

"I can do it myself," I tell her, but she shakes her head.

"Not this time. The gown is too big for you to reach your feet."

Great. More restrictions. There's no way I can fight in this.

I sit down, and she gently curves my foot into the slippers. She stands up and then glances at the vase on the table. She takes the small, colorful flowers and gestures for me to face the mirror. I do, and she gently places them into my hair. "Now you'll definitely stand out at the ball."

I smile and she kisses my forehead. "Go have fun and steal some hearts tonight."

We both turn as a knock sounds on the door. "That must be your escort." Quinn.

I look at her. "Do you mind opening the door? I need to take care of something first."

She nods and turns to move through the sitting room to open the door. When I'm sure that she's at a fair distance, I kneel down and take out a small sword, adding it to the holster at my thigh as well. It doesn't weigh much, so it shouldn't be much of a problem. I get up and walk to the door. Quinn is standing in the hallway. His blond hair shines in the light, and he's wearing a Mediterranean-blue tunic with black tights that make the blues of his eyes even brighter.

He looks at me, and his eyes widen as he smiles. "You look beautiful."

"Thank you. So do you."

He smiles. "Thank you."

We walk down toward the ballroom, my shoes clicking against the floor and making sounds that echo off the walls. The gown tickles my ankles and I wonder how the people in my village would react if they saw me now. A peasant at a royal ball. I press my hand against my dress to make sure the dagger and sword are still there; they are my only safety and there's no way I can run in this gown. We finally reach the doors, where dull music filters through.

Quinn asks me, "Are you ready?"

I take a deep breath. "Yes."

The guards open the doors for us, and immediately we are hit with the music of the orchestra above. A grand staircase leads down toward the ballroom, and soft laughter and light conversation fill the room. Nervousness rushes in. What if we don't find the stone? Everything will be for nothing.

"Hey," Quinn says, dragging my attention from the doors. "It'll be fine. We'll find it."

He gives a comforting smile that calms my nerves and I take a deep breath.

As we step into the ballroom, my breath escapes me. Walls adorned with gold soar to the ceiling high above. Leaves decorate the walls and a table set to the side with food. But what really catches my attention is the blend of colors as people dance and mingle.

I try to take it all in as we walk down the stairs. When we reach the dance floor, Quinn turns and looks at me. "Dance with me? You can look around and see if you can spot the stone, and use your tracking spell."

I nod and he takes my hand. The song playing ends and another slow melody begins. Quinn leads me to the dance floor and we soon fall into the familiar rhythm of dancing. I look into his eyes and smile. I wish I could just stay in his arms like this, not having a care in the world, but I'm here for something much more important. I break out of the trance and look at the dancers around us for anything that looks like it could be the stone.

"See anything?" Quinn asks after a while.

"No." I say frustrated.

"Use that tracking spell you were talking about, then."

I touch the stone hanging from my necklace and, in my mind, I whisper: *Find your other half.*

I wait for a few minutes, but nothing happens.

"Anything?" Quinn questions.

"Nothing. It's not here. If it's in the palace, it's not in the room right now."

"We should stay. Some people aren't even here yet."

"Okay," I say, but I already start to feel a sinking feeling in my stomach.

The song ends and we come to a halt. Quinn offers his arm and I take it. We walk off the dance floor and go back to where we had stood earlier.

"My, my, my. Do my eyes deceive me?" Quinn and I turn to the voice and see that it's coming from a short man who looks to be in his mid-thirties. Gaudy jewelry hangs from his neck, and his fingers glisten with more rings than I can count. His black eyes focus on us with scorn, and a nervous feeling settles in my stomach. I feel Quinn stiffen under my hand.

With barely veiled contempt, Quinn addresses the man. "Zelimer."

CHAPTER 37

QUINN

H E SMILES, REVEALING his signature gold teeth, and I try to keep my annoyance in check. He is probably here on a mission. I hate running into other assassins during my missions or while away from the Compound in general.

I grit my teeth hard when he turns his attention to Wren. His eyebrows rise into arches. "And who is this?"

Wren clenches my arm and I purse my lips.

"Fancy meeting you here," I say, hoping to take his attention away from Wren.

It works, and he looks at me again. "Interesting to see you here as well. What a pleasant surprise."

But his eyes say something totally different. Zelimer never liked me, not when I am only a few years more than half his age and still earning more missions than he does. He's one of the worst assassins. If his mission is to dispose of someone, he doesn't let them simply die a quick death.

He tortures them, even though he doesn't have to. He enjoys it. I was blackmailed into doing whatever Damien wants; he willingly does it.

"Long way from the Compound," he says, sneering. "Damien can't save you here."

I scoff. Damien wouldn't even attempt to save me. Not now, not ever. And Zelimer obviously underestimates what I'm capable of. Wren squeezes my arm.

"What's he talking about?"

I freeze. I forgot that she's next to me. "Nothing," I tell her softly, meeting her gaze.

I can tell by the look in her eyes that she doesn't believe me, but she doesn't push it further.

I look back at Zelimer and give him a stiff bow. "Pleasure meeting you." Sarcasm laces my voice. "But I promised her a drink."

We turn to go and my shoulders relax, but we don't take more than one step before his voice calls out again. "Scared?"

My hand clenches into a fist, and I gently move Wren's hand off my arm. I quickly turn back around and walk to him until we're almost touching. I lean down to look in his face and eyes. I lower my voice. "Never, and you know that. You can comfort yourself with these delusions you make in your mind, but you and I both know they're lies, and everyone else at the Compound knows too. I've earned those missions because, as much as you hate it, the truth is I am better than you."

His eyes widen in surprise, and I see fear in his eyes. I smirk, pull away, and walk back to Wren.

Her eyes are wide, and I inwardly cringe.

"What did you say to him?" she asks.

"Nothing."

Her lips turn into a thin line and I can tell she's upset, but, again, she doesn't push it. "Maybe, one day, you'll learn something called honesty," she says plainly, but those words are like a slap to my face.

We start walking, and spend most of our time in tense silence. We're standing near one of the pillars when, suddenly, one of the guards at the top of the stairs proclaims, "Announcing the Royal Family of Elrea." The doors open, and the Ashleighs in all their glory enter.

The room falls silent and everyone turns to watch the royal family. The king and queen enter first, their arms linked. Their crowns glisten under the chandeliers as they walk down the steps. The king wears a dark purple, velvet surcoat that's embroidered with what must be real gold, and a fur pelt is draped over his shoulder. Despite the festivities, he wears a grim look. The queen stands in sharp contrast with her soft expression, and she smiles at the crowd. She wears a long, golden gown of silk and a white crown rests on her head, sparkling. Behind them is the crown prince, Prince Sebastian. He looks around the room with excitement and a twinkle in his eyes. His gray tunic is obviously a sharp contrast to his mood. Next are Zayne and little Princess Rose. The princess is clothed in a beautiful pink gown and, like Wren, wears flowers in her hair. Roses. She clutches the sleeve of Zayne's green tunic, and he gently pries her hand off to hold it instead.

Everyone clears a path for the royal family and, as one, we all bow.

They slowly walk across the dance floor, and Zayne smiles at Wren and me as he passes, which causes the people who notice to give us curious looks. The royal family takes their places behind a long, rectangle table that is on a raised dais overlooking the crowd. The music starts again and people gradually begin to dance once more.

Wren and I roam throughout the grand ballroom and I keep my eyes out for anything unusual in the crowd. I feel a hand on my shoulder and turn to see Zayne, excitement in his eyes. "Did you find it yet?"

I shake my head. "Not yet, I'm afraid."

He frowns. "Okay, tell me when you do."

Just as he leaves, I feel Wren grow very still. I look to see her focusing on the queen. The blood rushes out of her face and my eyebrows bunch in concern. "What's wrong?"

She gulps and turns to face me. "The stone. I found it."

I mask my excitement. "Where?"

"It's on the queen's crown."

My eyes widen before I quickly mask it again. I squint at the queen's crown, and indeed, right there in the center is the small blue stone. I smile for show in case anyone is watching us and, out of the corner of my mouth, I ask, "How in the world are we going to get it?"

She lets out a deep sigh. "I have no idea. We can ask Zayne to get it for us."

"No." I shake my head. "I don't think you understand. Everyone knows about the stone on the crown of the Queen. It was her grandmother's."

"Yeah, but who do you think gave it to her grandmother? My family. To keep it safe, but now I need it back."

"She's not just going to hand it over."

"I know, but maybe she knows who my family is. Maybe she'll give it back."

"And she'll just believe that you're the Enchanters' Child?"

She shakes her head. "No, I can show her my magic."

"But you still don't have your magic, remember? You said you can get it back with the power the stone gives you, but you need the other half of the stone for that. Plus, you'll never get close enough to talk to her."

She looks at me, undeterred. "I have to try."

I let out a gentle sigh, knowing she's right.

CHAPTER 38

ZAYNE

I've ALWAYS HATED these events and the forced rules of etiquette we have to maintain. It is rare to see genuine people here because they are always trying to impress the royal family. I maneuver through the room brandishing a strained smile, talking to the people Father told me to speak with. Usually I am not so restless, but I am anxious to get to Wren and see if she has discovered where the other half of the Lochaere is.

Just as I spot another one of Father's friends that I must speak to, a hand grasps my arm. I tense, but when I turn to see who it is, I realize it's Quinn. The look in his eyes is full of excitement, and I know that they have found the other half. I follow him to the edge of the ballroom and spy Wren waiting for us.

"So, where is it?" I ask, looking around in excitement.

Wren looks at me and blurts out, "It's the stone on your mother's crown."

"What?" I ask, confused.

Wren explains what had happened, and slow realiza tion floods in.

"Okay, this is good. She's my mother. All we have to do is ask her, right?" I say finally.

"That's what I said, but are you sure she would part with it so easily?" Wren asks.

"I do admit that it will take some convincing on our part, but we can do it. Enjoy the rest of your night, and we'll talk to her tomorrow morning. The sooner we get the other half, the better," I finish. Quinn and Wren both agree, and I part from them to continue socializing.

The next morning, the three of us are in one of the sitting rooms in the castle, waiting for the queen. We agreed that I should be the one to take the lead, given that she is my mother. Wren is seated on one of the couches, while Quinn paces back and forth before the fireplace. I pick up a book to examine the cover, when the door swings open. I turn around to see my mother in the entryway and on her head is the crown, the blue Lochaere glowing slightly. When I look behind her, I am surprised to see that there are no guards escorting her. Wren jumps to her feet as Quinn stops pacing. We all bow and curtsy before rising again to meet her eye.

My mother looks at us with amusement.

"Oh, please. Those formalities aren't needed here."

She closes the door behind her and takes a seat on the couch that Wren had just been occupying.

"Please, sit," she says, gesturing to the couches while looking at Quinn and Wren. "I've been meaning to meet you all properly since the moment I heard he had brought you to the palace."

"Mother, there is some urgent business we need to discuss with you."

She waves her hand. "Whatever it is can wait a few minutes, can't it? I want to know more about your friends."

"I'm afraid it's of the utmost importance," I add.

She meets my gaze, and must have seen the urgency on my face, because she sighs and relents. "Very well. What is it?"

I gesture at Wren to speak, and she blinks at me before looking to my mother. "Your Majesty, my name is Wren and this is Quinn," she starts, and then explains the mission we are on and how it's linked to the deaths I was assigned to find the cause behind. The queen sends me a sharp look, only just realizing what I had gotten myself into.

"So, you're saying you're the daughter of the enchanters that gave mother the stone?"

Wren swallows and nods.

My mother pauses and looks down at her hands. "Okay, I'll give you the stone if you can prove to me that you are really who you say you are."

"By doing magic?" Wren asks.

The queen nods.

"Your Majesty, I'm afraid my magic is drained at the moment, but if I have the other half of the Lochaere, I will be able to show you."

The queen frowns. "Very well."

She reaches above her head and slowly takes off the

crown. She gently removes the stone from the small hook it is dangling on and hands it to Wren. Mother watches with curiosity as Wren carefully receives the stone. All our eyes train on Wren with bated breath as she lifts the stone to the other half of the Lochaere on her necklace. The opposing half fits perfectly, and for an instant, nothing happens. Then the stone starts to glow blue.

I watch in amazement as the seam that indicates where the stones had parted begins to glow a hot white color, as it meshes the two pieces together. The shining gradually recedes to reveal the Lochaere in its entirety. The necklace lies on Wren's throat, and it's hard to believe it holds so much power. Wren lets out a laugh of relief and amazement before she grabs a hold of the stone and begins to murmur. Suddenly, she gasps, and then a wide smile graces her face.

"I can feel my magic again."

She looks down at her hands and starts to mutter again. A book that lies on the table in front of the couch rises and hovers in the air for a couple of seconds, before it is gently placed on the table again.

Mother stares at the book for a long moment before looking up at Wren. "Be careful what you do with that stone. It was given to me to ensure that it doesn't fall into the wrong hands."

Wren bows her head. "I will, Your Majesty."

"Very well. Good luck to you all."

She rises to her full height and strides toward me, then gently lays her hand on my arm. "Be safe, Zayne. Your father told me how he plans for you to stay here, but we both know you are leaving. All I ask is for you to come back alive." She kisses me on the cheek and leaves the room.

As the door closes behind her, we all stare at the necklace. We finally had the whole piece. "It kick-started your magic." We can enter the forest.

"So, what now?" Quinn asks.

"We leave. We don't have any time to waste," I speak up.

Wren looks at Quinn. "Zayne is right. We'll leave in two hours, so you can say goodbye to your family, Zayne. When it's time, we'll meet at the main entrance of the palace."

I find my siblings and my mother, and tell them goodbye. I consider not telling my father, but I must, or there will be severe consequences. I hesitate before knocking on my father's door.

I hear his voice. "Come in."

I take a deep breath before pushing open the door. My father looks up at me before turning his attention back to the papers on his desk.

"What is it?" he asks, distracted.

"I just wanted to inform you that I'm leaving."

He looks at me then, a wrinkle forming between his eyebrows. "What do you mean?"

"I found the cause for the deaths, and I'm leaving to take care of it."

His gaze hardens. "I thought we agreed that you were staying here."

"Father, with all due respect, I think this is what I'm meant to do. My duty. This royal life, it isn't for me."

"You better wish nobody else hears you saying that."

"I'm going," I repeat. "There are lives at stake if I do not."

For a second, I see his eyes soften. "You better come right back after and we'll have a talk."

I give him a nod, relieved.

As I turn to leave, he speaks up. "And Zayne?"

I turn.

"Be safe," he says finally.

I give him a gentle smile before leaving the room.

CHAPTER 39

WREN

I MEET UP WITH Zayne and Quinn at the palace
entrance, but as we turn to leave, we notice a shadow
near the exit. Zayne immediately draws out his sword
in caution as the figure steps out into the light.

"Raulin?" Zayne asks, confused, as he lowers his
sword.

The nice man that I met in the training room is
replaced with someone who wants to kill us. He steps
toward us in anger, and that's when I notice the glint of a
sword in his hand. Just as warning bells ring in my mind,
my Lochaere starts to glow a bright blue.

"Zayne." I say slowly. "Get back."

He glances at my necklace before looking back at
Raulin in confusion. "Raulin? No, it's not possible."

"Zayne, I think you should listen to Wren," Quinn
says cautiously.

With Zayne turned to look at us, Quinn and I watch

as Raulin lifts the sword in his hand. I freeze, and in the next second, Quinn pulls out his own sword and blocks Raulin's blow before it can hit Zayne.

Zayne wheels around, bearing an expression of shock and hurt toward his friend. He's about to open his mouth to speak when I see the symbol of a triangle and arrow etched into Raulin's forearm. I let out a gasp. Zayne and Quinn's eyes draw to where I'm looking.

Their faces grow pale, and Zayne whispers, "How did they find us?"

Before anyone can speak, Raulin grabs Zayne. There's no time to react, and I see a flash of silver as he quickly stabs Zayne in the stomach. Quinn lets out a shout of horror. I hastily conjure up a stunning spell, and throw it at Raulin. Until we can come up with a way to get rid of the spell of the Sorcerer on him, this is the best course of action. I don't think anyone will appreciate it if we kill him. Raulin quickly falls to the ground, as Zayne collapses with a groan.

Quinn rushes to Zayne's side, and a couple of soldiers rush toward us, having noticed the commotion before I can attempt to heal Zayne on my own. I quickly tell them that Raulin has had too much drink and attacked the prince. The soldiers' eyes reflect shock at what their comrade has done, before they quickly take him to the dungeons under the castle. I feel a jab of guilt; it isn't his fault, but instead the mark of the Sorcerer. There is nothing we can do now; the mark is forever etched into his skin.

I help Quinn to carry Zayne to the infirmary. The

pain must have rendered him unconscious and the nurse, a woman in her late fifties with a stern look on her face, mutters, "What is it with you all getting hurt so much?"

She arranges an area for the prince in one of the private infirmary rooms in the back. We stand beside the bed as she assesses his wounds. If I can get Zayne alone, I can heal his wound with magic, but I can't do it with the nurse here.

"How bad is it?" I hold my breath.

"Not good, but he'll survive," she says with a smile.

Just as she says that, a group of soldiers storm into the room.

"What's all this?" the nurse demands as she stands up, placing her hands on her hips.

One of the soldiers steps forward. "Due to the attack, we are required to guard the prince and ensure his safety while he's recovering." He then looks at Quinn and I with an apologetic look. "That means only guards and a nurse in the room."

I try to protest, but Quinn lays a hand on my shoulder and squeezes, as if to assure me it's okay.

"That's fine," he tells the soldiers before leading me out of the room. He closes the door and says, "We can't do anything about it now, Wren."

"But I might be able to heal him with my magic if I just get him alone!"

"Wren. We can't do anything about it right now. Let's go outside and get some fresh air. We'll think of something when we get back."

As we leave the room, I look at him with confusion and worry.

"I don't understand," I say slowly. "How did the Sorcerer find us?"

"I don't have the answer to that, I'm afraid."

CHAPTER 40

ZAYNE

I SLOWLY OPEN MY eyes and wince as the light from the window blinds me. When my vision clears, I find myself in an unfamiliar bed within an unfamiliar room. I squint in confusion, and then remember what had happened. Raulin. The Sorcerer's sign. The pain in my abdomen. I sit up in a rush as everything comes back to me. I know Raulin wasn't himself when he attacked us; it was the symbol. But who put it on him?

As my mind starts to clear, I realize that there are guards lining the walls.

"What's this?" I ask, confused.

"Because of the attack, we're required to stay here until you have recovered, Your Highness," says one of the guards.

"On whose order?" I demand.

"Your brother's, Your Highness."

I fall back against the mattress with a sigh of frustration and squeeze my eyes shut. We were supposed to be on our way to the forest by now. Every minute spent here is a minute wasted.

All of a sudden, I feel a rumble as the bed trembles slightly. The guards look at each other in confusion before I hear a commotion outside the room.

A fresh guard quickly rushes in looking at the soldier that had been talking to me. "Henry, there's been an explosion on the other side of the castle. Everyone is required to report there immediately."

"What about the prince?" Henry asks.

The messenger looks at me, unsure.

The guard sighs and points to a soldier waiting in the corner of the room. "Merek, you stay. The rest of you, follow me," he says and the others obey, draining from the room.

Merek nods at me before settling back into his corner. I frown, thinking about what may have caused the explosion, puzzling over the timing of it. I lean back against the pillows and wonder when Quinn and Wren will come, just as I hear the door open. I look up in relief, expecting to see them, but it's not their faces that appear through the entryway.

I sit up once again in confusion. "Lucas?"

He gives me a curt nod. "Zayne."

"What are you doing here?"

Lucas' face suddenly turns hostile. "I'm afraid you're about to find out, little prince."

Merek steps forward cautiously, and it's only when he gets too close that I notice the dagger in Lucas' hand. I let out a shout of warning, but it's too late. Merek stumbles to the floor with a grunt of pain and Lucas starts to approach me. I stretch out my arm to try and reach my own dagger on the small table beside my bed, but a sharp pain from the stab wound paralyzes me.

"I didn't want to have to do this, you know. Hurt anybody else. If only Raulin had succeeded in his task, then we wouldn't be in this situation."

I look at him with horror. "What have you done?"

"What I must do," he says with conviction. "Ordinary people aren't safe in a world with magic. The Sorcerer offered me magic, power."

"And you think he's actually going to keep his word?" I spit out.

"After what I'm about to do, yes," he says and gives me a sickly smile. I once again try to slowly reach toward my dagger as I try to conceal the pain behind a neutral mask.

As he approaches even closer, I start to speak, in hopes of distracting him. "The Dark Sorcerer is not going to give you any magic, Lucas. You are foolish to think otherwise."

Lucas looks at me with the eyes of a man drunk on the possibility of power, and I wonder how I hadn't seen it before. His mouth turns into a snarl. "You don't know what you're talking about."

"You haven't seen the type of things that he's capable of. A man like that wouldn't be willing to give magic to another," I say, begging him to understand.

For a second, I see a glimpse of doubt in his eyes, before they harden once more. My stomach turns sour as he lifts his arm, prepared to stab me, just as I feel the dagger's hilt in the palm of my hand. Before he has time to land the blow, I pierce my dagger into his stomach, shouting in pain as the stiches of my wound break loose. Lucas staggers back in agony, looking down with shock at the dagger now protruding from his stomach.

He stumbles forward to take another strike at me when the door opens, and Wren and Quinn step in, laughing at something one of them said. They look up and their expressions slowly change into shock as their eyes land on us – on the dagger in Lucas' hand. Quinn is the first one to react and, before I can blink, a dagger flies past my face, hitting Lucas in the chest. Lucas chokes out a sound as he crumbles to the floor and I look away with a grimace. If the Dark Sorcerer contacted Lucas about us, I wonder how deep his magic actually runs.

Wren steps up to me, her face pale. "Zayne, are you okay?"

I nod, numbly. "Yeah, yeah, I'm fine."

Quinn looks at Lucas with a frown. "Now we know how Raulin got the mark."

I grit my teeth in anger. I had trusted Lucas and considered him one of my closest companions.

"Zayne! Your wound!" Wren exclaims.

I look down to see a pool of red seeping through my tunic and, suddenly, the pain rushes back. I quickly recount what had happened to Wren and Quinn, and Wren speaks up when I finish.

"I could try healing your wound. Then you would be good as new. Although I must warn you, it might hurt a little," she says with a gentle smile.

My eyebrows rise in interest and I nod. She places her hands over the tunic where my wound is and starts to mutter another one of her spells. Immediately, the Lochaere starts to glow a faint blue and a similar light appears beneath her hands. I wince at the quick sting that comes as my skin begins to knit itself together, but it's nothing compared to when I first received the injury.

Minutes later, the light starts to fade and Wren takes her hand away from my tunic.

"It should be healed now," she says, and I gingerly lift up the material to find that the skin has lost any traces of the stab wound.

Quinn looks at the Lucas' body grimly and then turns to us. "We have to leave as quickly as we can. We don't know if he's the only one that the Dark Sorcerer is in contact with; it's too dangerous here."

I slowly twist my body to see if there's any lingering pain. When I feel nothing, I quickly rise from the bed and move to exit the room, telling the others to get their bags and meet at Quinn's room as soon as possible. This trip is *filled* with near-death experiences.

CHAPTER 41

WREN

BEFORE I KNOW it, we enter the forest, and my mind immediately wanders to my run-in with the fairies the previous night. I shiver as I think about how angry they were.

Quinn leads us at the front, and after hours of walking, we finally stop for the night after we check to ensure it's safe. Just as we lay our bags down, Zayne announces that he's going to go find some wood, and leaves the clearing. I pick up my satchel to drink another vial, but pause when I realize I have run out. Too exhausted to make another one from the plant, I turn to Quinn and hold up the vial.

Quinn nods, understanding. "It's in my satchel."

I walk over to the bag and reach inside to find his vial, but I stop short when I see something that makes my blood run cold. I remain silent, staring at his bag. Quinn notices my pause, and he looks at me in confusion. "Wren?"

I stand up, the black mask dangling from my finger-tips. "What is this?" I know very well what it is, but I don't understand what it's doing in Quinn's bag.

I watch Quinn's face pale, and I feel dread. "I can explain," he says, looking at me with panic in his eyes – and that's how I know.

"Y- you're…" I trailed off, not finishing the sentence. He is the Black Assassin. Tears fill up in my eyes and, for the first time when I look at him, I feel a twinge of fear. I think about all the moments he had me alone, and a tear slides down my face.

Oh, how stupid of me. All this time, I was thinking I was careful and that I was escaping all the bounty hunt-ers and assassins after me, and here was one of the people I was starting to trust the most in the world, who is, in reality, the most dangerous assassin and bounty hunter of them all.

Anger rushes through me, and I can feel my face flush. "How could you?" A sudden thought hits me and I gasp. "Were you sent for me?"

"Wren," he chokes out and reaches towards me.

"Answer the question." I grit out in anger.

When he remains silent, that's when I know. I flinch as I see pain in his eyes. "I trusted you. I thought you were like me."

"Wren, hear me out," Quinn begs. "Once I got to know you, I knew I couldn't hurt you." I flinch again, but he rushes ahead, trying to explain. "You made me realize that I could be a better person."

"That was before I knew who you were." Quinn steps

back like I slapped his face and I feel a stab of guilt. I grow angrier; I shouldn't feel guilty for accusing him. "Just leave me alone," I whisper out as my voice breaks, the fight leaving me.

Remorse is etched across his face and there is a sheen in his eyes. If it was anyone else, I would think those were tears, but the Black Assassin doesn't cry and this is an act, tears included.

I look down, gathering my emotions, and look up as I feel my magic at my fingertips, urging me to get rid of the threat, but he's gone. I look at the ground to see that he has taken his things with him, and it seems like he hasn't even been there in the first place. I feel my face crumble as the numbing starts to fade away and a sharp pain blooms in my chest. I fall to the ground and put my face in my hands, and then weep.

CHAPTER 42

ZAYNE

I START TO HEAD back to the clearing, absently
humming a song. Music has a way of grounding me,
and I need it now more than ever, because I know
what's ahead of us. We are really doing it, going into
the Forest of Alberich, and then there's no turning back.
Despite that, however, I know that I won't back down,
because I can't just walk away from this. If we actually
stop the Sorcerer, that means no more deaths and, in a
way, we will be avenging the ones he's already killed.

I don't know if the faces of those who died will ever
escape me, but it will put my mind at ease if the Sorcerer
gets what is coming to him. As I approach the clearing,
I hear the faint sound of sobbing, and my heart stops. I
pick up the pace while trying to balance the wood in my
arms, but when I see Wren crying on the ground, I drop
the logs everywhere and they roll in all directions. Wren

doesn't look up from where she is, and I rush to her in worry.

"Wren? What's wrong? Where's Quinn?"

I touch her shoulder and lean back in surprise as I see her splotchy face. Her eyes hold an immense sadness and betrayal.

"Wren?" I repeat.

She sobs and puts her head on my shoulder. "I have no more brains than a stone, Zayne. I can't believe I was so blind."

Confused, I look down at her. "What are you talking about?"

"He lied to us."

"Who?" I wasn't going to get anything out of her at this point. "Wren, take a slow breath and tell me what happened."

She stills before I feel her taking in a large breath. She releases it as she steps back and I see that, at least, the tears have stopped. She grits her teeth before she talks, and what she says leaves me in shock.

"Quinn. He- I still can't believe it." She shakes her head before continuing, "He's the Black Assassin, Zayne. He was sent to kill me or capture me." She sniffs. "He betrayed us."

My jaw drops, and I try to wrap my mind around what she just told me. I feel anger snake through me, even as I try to push it down.

"Are you sure?" I stutter.

A tear runs down Wren's face, and she rises and steps aside. "See for yourself." There, lying in the grass, is the infamous mask of the Black Assassin. It gleams in the sunlight, as if it is taunting us.

"But I can't believe he would do that. We trusted him... He was a friend."

"Yeah? Well, it was all an act, apparently." Wren's voice is laced with anger, and I don't blame her; I feel the same way. No one likes being betrayed and feeling like a fool for considering someone an ally just to be stabbed in the back. Wren jerks her satchel onto her back, and she starts walking into the forest without looking back at me.

"Come on, let's go."

I knew there was something dangerous about Quinn when I first met him, but after a while, I started to think that I was wrong. I had let my guard down and had started to consider him trustworthy. And I don't trust people unless they prove that they are worth being trusted in the first place. However, even as I believe this, one thought stays with me as I follow Wren.

Quinn had plenty of opportunities to hurt or kidnap Wren. So, then, why didn't he?

We walk into the forest, and immediately an intense feeling of silence comes down on us. Everything seems to go quiet, and the only sounds are our own. The entire environment starts to shift as green grass makes way for brown, and life seems to die right in front of my eyes. Fear threatens to make me immobile, but I force my feet to keep moving forward.

"Well, can't turn back now," Wren says, trying to sound flippant, but her voice is strained. She barely even said the words, yet it sounded as though she was shouting.

I look around and take in the black tree branches that seem as if they are reaching for us. The leaves block out the sunlight, enveloping the earth with muted darkness. The grass comes up to my ankles, and the dirt makes my boots slowly sink in.

I suddenly feel an errant sensation and I halt. "Wren."

She looks back, her body rigid. She tilts her head in question and I put my finger to my mouth in a gesture to stay silent. I'm tense as I try to observe the shadows from the corners of my eyes. As I'm looking, the Lochaere around Wren's neck starts to glow. Wren looks down and realization makes her pale face turn to gray, almost matching her eyes, but she says nothing.

We are being watched.

"Come toward me, slowly," I say quietly, and Wren begins to tremble as she carefully does so.

I try to not let fear consume me, but a little fear is a good thing. It sharpens my senses and makes me act. I just have to use it wisely. Wren is two feet away from me when she steps on a twig. I flinch and, immediately, one of the shadows lunges at us. I turn toward the movement in a fighting stance, but I'm not prepared for what I see.

The creature in front of us is hardly discernible as it approaches, but its size is astounding. It towers above us, as tall as the trees, and it seems to take up most of the small clearing. The Lochaere becomes the brightest I've ever seen it as the creature grows nearer, and slowly the features of the beast are unmasked. Gnarled black skin gleams first as the light slowly creeps its way up to the creature's face. I only see a glimpse of yellow eyes before it's barreling toward us.

I leap to the side and break into run. I pass Wren, who is frozen in shock, and I grab her arm as we sprint out of the clearing together. Fear makes us run fast, and we sprint until our chests burn and our throats ache. My legs feel like rubber, but still we keep running as adrenaline shoots through us.

I lose track of time and only come to a stop when we reach a cliff. I collapse onto my back and look up at the sky, trying to catch my breath. I close my eyes, but in my mind, I can see the beast staring back at me. To distract myself, I turn my head to the side and spy Wren mirroring my position as she tries to calm herself. The Lochaere at her throat is dim now, but there is still a slight glow to it.

"Your potion isn't going to help us now, Wren," I say once I can breathe. "This forest is crawling with monsters."

She is silent and I watch her cautiously, worried. She is now sitting up, and she stares into the distance with an expression of awe. "Zayne, look," she says and points ahead. I gaze beyond the cliff.

A river snakes across the land and, as I look past it, I see what has captured Wren's attention. There, in the middle of the forest, lies a dark, red tower, the bottom half lost in the trees below. The tower itself appears to spiral around itself, but there are no windows. It lets out a malicious, dark power, and it almost feels like it is seeping into my skin, making me want to scrub the layers away. At the top, a part seems to jut out, and it appears to be a kind of balcony. As I watch it, I think I see a figure standing there watching us, but when I blink, the shadow is gone.

"That's got to be where the Sorcerer is, Zayne."

I'm speechless. What exactly are we up against?

CHAPTER 43

QUINN

I STAY IN THE trees, long after Zayne and Wren enter the Forest of Alberich.

Just leave me alone.

Wren's voice echoes in my mind as I try to disregard the sharp pain in my chest. Attempting to ignore the guilt threatening to crush me, I force myself to move. I lower myself onto the ground, wondering what I should do, but then I get an idea. Even though she hates me, I have to make sure Wren is safe. I pick up my satchel, determination on my face, and walk in the opposite way of the dark forest.

I soon become enveloped in the trees, and to someone watching, it might seem that I'm lost. The path to where I aim to go is confusing and with good reason. The people I want to find don't want to be found. I follow a subtle path and hear a small rustle in the trees. Expectantly, I look up, and staring back is a young, scrawny boy blinking at me.

His olive skin glistens in the sun like gold, despite the dirt covering him, and his green eyes reflect the forest, shining like beacons.

I slowly nod at him, and he jerks away to run along the branch and out of sight. I must be getting nearer. I pause shortly after and stop underneath a tree. I quickly climb up the trunk and into the heavy branches, and start running from tree to tree like the boy did. Gradually, structures in the trees start to appear, and before long, a village is in view. Small huts lean against various thick branches, and some bridges connect those that are too far away to be leapt across. I cautiously step onto one of the platforms, but immediately, I feel a knife at my throat. I wince and hold up my hands.

"Don't move," a low voice growls in my ear.

A hand shoves me forward, and we start walking across the platform. He brings me to a halt in the middle of it, and four figures materialize from the shadows. They all have the same olive skin like the boy I had seen earlier. Each wears a uniform of brown with a golden leaf patch, the symbol of the tree people, on their sleeves. Guards.

A woman with red hair steps up, and her onyx eyes stare at me with suspicion. "What is your business here? You better have a good reason for your trespassing," she says with a powerful voice, and if I were anyone else, I would be scared. Instead, I lift my chin and look her in the eyes.

"I'm here to see Tristan."

She takes another step forward and pulls her sword out. "Why?"

I don't look at the sword and instead raise my eyebrow. "I can't tell you that."

Her eyes start to fill with anger and suspicion, and she opens her mouth like she's prepared to say something, but before she can, a voice rings out over us. "Leave him, Friya. He isn't going to bring us any harm."

I frown, insulted. I thought I was more intimidating.

The guards shift positions, and standing there is a person I never thought I would see again. Tristan is the only person I have ever let get close to me. I never had that many friends, but she was from the same village as I, and both our families were killed by the Sorcerer.

Damien had taken us both in, and we were raised under his thumb. Her raven hair and blue eyes helped her on numerous missions. She had many people wrapped around her finger and used them to get things that were beneficial for Damien. We would go on missions together, sometimes, and she would always be the charmer. I was more intimidating at the start, and filled with hate; people didn't approach me. But our friendship didn't last long, and all because I'm a selfish lowlife.

But you've changed, a voice tries to say in my mind and, in a way, I have changed, but I can't let Tristan think I'm going soft. She'll use it to her advantage.

I slip my face into the cold mask that I always wore, before I met Wren and Zayne.

Tristan watches me quietly, and her face shows nothing. I stare back at her and take in how much she's changed since I last saw her years ago. Her cheeks have sunken in, making the bones of her face prominent. The eyes staring back at me now are not filled with the warmth that used to be there and are instead filled with darkness.

Finally, she breaks the silence. "I thought I told you that if I ever saw you again, I would kill you myself."

I hide the regret and sadness that threatens to show on my face. I hate that she's nothing like the best friend I used to know, and I hate that I'm the reason for it. I ruin all the relationships that come into my life. It's something that's inevitable because of who I am. "I need your help," I say carefully.

She lets out a scoff of disbelief. "Why in the world would you need my help?"

I let out a slow breath, hoping I'm not making a mistake. "I need to get into the Sorcerer's tower."

"What?" Her eyes slowly fill with understanding. "You can't kill him. It's not possible.

I pause, not wanting to give Wren away to her. "I know someone."

She cocks her head in curiosity. "Who?"

I look at her guards, hoping she thinks the reason I don't want to tell her is because we have an audience.

Tristan closes her eyes and seems to mumble to herself, before latching her blue eyes onto mine. "Then I'm coming."

What? "Really?" I didn't really expect her to even agree, let alone that quickly. Suspicion wraps around me and I squint at her. "Why?"

She rolls her eyes in exasperation. "As much as I don't want to be with you longer than I have to, the Sorcerer killed my parents."

I run my hand through my hair, suddenly anxious. I've never been in a position where my life is in the hands of someone else, but I need her to get me through the forest alive. No one knows the forest like she does. I'm about to back out, when I think about Wren and Zayne. I can't leave them by themselves to fight the Sorcerer. I need to be there to make sure that they succeed. I'll leave after that, even if it breaks my heart.

I smirk, trying to hide my thoughts. "Well, then, let's go."

CHAPTER 44

WREN

SEEING THE SORCERER'S tower reminds me of what we're going up against. I try to banish thoughts of doubt by reminding myself that I'm the Enchanters' Child, but it's not working. That night, hidden behind some bushes, I take out my mother's book for the first time. I hug it to my chest, hoping for some comfort, and blink away tears that threaten to escape. I sneak a look at Zayne, who seems to be asleep, before tentatively opening the book. My mother's perfume wafts from the pages and, for the first time when thinking about my mother, I smile.

I flip through the book before landing on a familiar page. Staring back at me is my favorite story, the one I made my mother read me every night before I went to sleep. This story is different, not like the rest of the book that is about the dark creatures which lurk around. There was comfort to be found in thinking that maybe something could defeat the creatures.

When I was a child, however, I was never scared of the monsters in my mother's stories, but that was before I saw them in real life. I think that, in a way, my mother knew something might happen and that I had to be prepared. This story, in particular, is about a prince who had heard there was a Ravager in the forest surrounding his father's kingdom. A Ravager is a creature of darkness that devastates homes and consumes the souls of those it finds. The Ravager had been attacking the villages on the outskirts of the kingdom.

Many people tried to capture the Ravager and bring an end to the deaths. The ruler of the kingdom had even sent his best soldiers to kill the beast, but none succeeded, for the beast kept escaping their clutches. The king soon gave up and told the villagers they had to deal with the problem themselves. The situation began to get worse and, soon, the villagers started placing blame on the king for their problems. As stories began to circulate of usurping the throne, the prince knew he had to do something. So, he went to the forest, bow and arrow in hand, to hunt the beast himself.

He started walking through the forest, hoping to catch sight of the Ravager, but instead ran into something far more magical. He found an Essence. It's said that this is the first and only time an Essence made itself known to another living being. According to legend, Essences are the only truly pure things in the world, composed of blue vapors in human form. Before King Alberich banned magic, they were a common symbol of hope and goodness.

The Essence approached the prince and said that there was only one way to be rid of the Ravager. The prince responded that he'd do anything. The Essence explained that it would give him what he needed to kill the great monster, but it required a sacrifice. The prince agreed and the Essence gave him magic. The first Arobol.

The prince used his magic to defeat the beast, and the Ravager vanished like shadows retreating when there is light. However, soon, the magic was too much for him and he suffered. He couldn't control it, and it became harder for him to hide his abilities. When the king found out, he banished his son, saying that he had dabbled with dark magic. So, the son left and went to the forest where he had met the Essence. He called out to it for weeks and, finally, it appeared. The Essence taught him how to control his abilities and told him that the magic would pass down for generations. His line would now be responsible for keeping the world safe from those who misused magic. So, while he lost his family, he had saved the lives of those living in the villages of his kingdom.

I pause. *He had to make a sacrifice. The Ravager vanished like shadows retreating when there is light.* A careful smile spreads across my face, as a plan starts to come together.

Zayne and I move cautiously as we make our way to the tower. Minutes of silence pass before Zayne speaks up.

"Are we ever going to talk about it?"

I look around, guardedly checking to see if we're safe. "Talk about what?" I ask, distracted. Zayne doesn't say anything and I look at him. "Zayne?"

He pauses, and then says, "Quinn."

I flinch. "There's nothing to talk about. He wasn't who we thought he was."

"Yes but-" he interjects and I cut him off.

"No 'buts,' Zayne. Quinn lied to us. For goodness sake, he's an assassin."

"I understand but…" I face him to protest, but his expression tells me to stop talking. "If he wanted to kidnap you, he would have, Wren. He's the Black Assassin; it wouldn't have taken him this long just to complete his mission."

I open my mouth to argue, but the words get stuck to the back of my throat as I stare at the scene in front of us. Meradas. Hundreds of miniature, translucent creatures fly softly above us, moving as if they're swimming through the air. Small wings, absent of feathers, sprout from their backs and small tails, each ending with the shape of a diamond, swishing back and forth in a hypnotic motion. Small hearts glow red inside them as their skin radiates with interchanging colors that set the sky into a mirage of hues. The Meradas move in a chaotic dance.

One drifts away from the others and slowly floats toward to me. I hold my breath in awe as a large pair of ultramarine eyes stare at me in curiosity. The Merada tilts its head at me for a moment before jerking it back and flying back to its kind.

I think back to the page in my mother's book, with a picture of a Merada etched on it. Meradas are said to have a connection with the magical and the natural world. They're thought to be extinct, according to the book, but clearly this forest is home to a countless number of them. I feel excitement and apprehension as I wonder what else is in this forest, and what else is waiting to be discovered. But I grow sober when I think about the mission we have come here to complete. The first objective is killing the Sorcerer, but for now, I enjoy the moment. I smile as I look at the Meradas and then at Zayne.

A horde of Meradas fly in circles around him, while some perch on his shoulders. He turns around slowly in awe, his eyes filled with tears of wonder, his mouth open slightly. I watch, surprised, and look at Zayne carefully. I think back to how he smelled the dreadful aroma of the potion. He has more magic in him that I thought; his connection with the Meradas is evidence of that.

I tilt my head in confusion. Someone with this degree of magic shouldn't have been dormant so long. I smile gently as I think about teaching him how to use his magic, should there be a chance that it makes an appearance. I keep this to myself, however, afraid of how he will react if he knows what I am thinking.

"Not everything magical is malicious," I say softly, and Zayne slowly nods in agreement.

Reluctantly, we leave the Meradas behind as we continue on our way. Strangely, we don't encounter any other creatures and don't have any trouble, but I have a constant feeling that we're being watched. For a second, I wonder if the creatures are under the Sorcerer's influence, but it dawns on me that I haven't seen a symbol on any of them. Is there a chance that he doesn't control them? The thought gives me hope, and I smile.

Zayne puts a hand on my shoulder, and it shakes me from my thoughts. I raise my eyebrows in question. He taps his ear and I strain to hear what he's indicating. That's when I catch the sound of rushing water. We look at each other and smile.

"We must be on the right track. I saw a river between us and the tower when we were on the cliff. Do you know what this means?" he says with nervous excitement, but continues without waiting for my answer. "We're halfway there."

We continue trekking and soon the river comes into view. A soft gasp escapes me as I stare at the water rushing by us. This isn't like any river I've ever seen before. The waters twist and weave around and through each other, as though the river itself is alive. It's so clear that I can see tiny creatures resembling fish navigating the waves to reach their destinations. Beyond the river are strands of grass that tower over us, giving off the illusion that we've shrunk.

"Do you have any idea how to get across?" Zayne inquires, and I bite my lip as I try to think of a solution. The waves are powerful and can easily sweep us downstream, taking us off course, so that isn't an option.

An idea begins to take shape in my mind. Inhaling a small breath, I absorb the energy coming from the Lochaere and put my attention on the spell. Slowly but steadily, a delicate bridge appears, crossing the river. I smile at Zayne and walk up to the fabricated structure. Yet, before I can place my foot on it, it shimmers and then fades into nothing. Shocked, I step back in confusion.

"Why did it disappear?" Zayne looks in concern at where the bridge had been just seconds ago.

Understanding dawns upon me. I shake my head at my daftness. "The woods don't allow anything made by an Arobol to stake a claim on the land. It's the land's way of making sure that everything stays the way it is."

Zayne tilts his head. "Then how did the Sorcerer create his tower?"

I frown. "There's more to this than meets the eye."

Zayne puts his hands on his hips and looks around, appearing lost. "Well, what are we going to do now?"

A slow plan starts to knit together in my mind. "I have an idea, but there's a chance for casualties."

"Like what?"

"Death?" I wince.

Zayne pauses. "This entire trip has been full of possibilities for death," he finally says. "What are you thinking?"

"I can levitate myself to the other side, and then I can levitate you, but the spell is hard. I can only levitate you for a short amount of time and it takes a lot of effort."

Zayne leans to the right and looks at the river behind me before returning to an upright position. "I've always wanted to fly."

"Wait, what?" I look at him, surprised. "Are you sure?"

He nods and I take a deep breath. Turning, I face the river.

Can't mess up now. I concentrate and slowly conjure up the spell. A slow, burning sensation begins where the Lochaere rests on my neck and it gradually spreads through my body. Steadily, a blue glow envelops my hands, and I feel the earth give way to air. I look down and see that I'm hovering two feet above the ground. I let out a laugh of relief and glance at Zayne.

Zayne stares at me with concern. "Are you sure you want to do this?"

I smile at him. "I've always wanted to fly too," I say, echoing his words back at him. I turn away and inhale a deep breath before rising up a few more feet. As I cautiously near the river, water sprays my face, and if I wasn't so frightened of falling, I might have enjoyed the moment.

I'm halfway across the river, my heart in my throat, when exhaustion hits like a horse trampling me beneath its feet - and I lose control. I scream as I fall toward the rushing river and shield my face, preparing for an onslaught of water. Instead, I feel a jarring lurch that makes me grit my teeth, and when I open my eyes, I find myself hovering above the water. I let out a shaky breath and slowly inch my way to the other side, this time attempting not to use as much energy. I almost cry with relief when I collapse into the grass. I brush the twigs off of my clothes and stand up, looking to see Zayne on the other side, his face pale.

"I thought you were going to die!" He shouts across.

I wince. "You're next!" I shout back.

"I'm second-guessing my decision."

"Too late for that. Are you ready?"

Zayne looks at the sky and mutters something before leveling his gaze at me. He nods, and I clench my fists to conjure up the spell, but before I can, a dark shadow looms over me. Confused, I turn around and my jaw opens. The one creature I hoped I would never encounter stands before me. A Ravager.

Before I can make a move to defend myself, it pounces and sinks its teeth into my arm. The last thing I hear are Zayne's shouts as everything fades to darkness.

CHAPTER 45

ZAYNE

PANIC STRIKES ME as I see the black creature looming over Wren, who lies unconscious at its feet. My throat closes up as I take in its features. It resembles a black panther, but thrice the size. Its green eyes flash up at me before looking at Wren, and that's when I notice the glowing, green symbol on its shoulder that flashes like a beacon. The Sorcerer.

As much as I want to scream, no sounds come out of my mouth as the creature bites Wren's shirt and flings her onto its back. Frustrated with helplessness and numb with shock, I sink to my knees as the creature walks away, and I wonder what we are going to do now.

Hours later, after I had tried and failed to determine a way to cross the river, I give up and sit down on a log. *Wren is on the other side of the river. She has been captured, and there's nothing I can do about it.*

Hours have passed, like silent, empty cavers. I've been

lost in silence. But the next morning, the sound of a twig snapping echoes through the silence, and I freeze. It could just be an innocent woodland creature, but I seriously doubt it. I slowly look around the forest for anything moving. It was bad enough when I was with Wren, but it's worse with no one by my side.

"Zayne," a voice behind me says out of nowhere.

Panic and fear rush through me, and I swivel around. Standing there is Quinn. Black circles under his eyes now mar his face, and exhaustion makes him look years older. I look into his eyes and I almost feel pity when I see the wild desperation there. His blond hair is in disarray. He looks like a drowning man. I still can't believe it, that he could betray us and that he was the Black Assassin.

Anger washes over me. "What are you doing here? I should run you through with my sword."

He brings up his hands, and I see that they're shaking. "Please," he whispers. "Hear me out."

I squint. "Are you mad? Why in the world would I do that?"

Suddenly, Quinn's eyebrows pull together and he whips his head back and forth as if he's searching for something. He looks at me then with confusion on his face. "W- where's Wren?"

I inwardly flinch. "Why would I tell you?"

He growls in frustration. "I'm not going to kill her. I would never."

I raise my eyebrows. "Your reputation begs to differ."

"Look, I know nothing I say will make this better, but

after I found out she was the Enchanters' Child, once I got to know her, I knew I couldn't kill her."

"How can I believe you? You've ended thousands of lives like it's nothing."

Anger shows in his eyes. "Like it's nothing? You think that all those deaths don't haunt me every second of my life? Even sleep isn't a reprieve. You think that I kill people because I enjoy it?" he shouts. "He has my sister! I have no choice!"

Raw pain shows in his voice, and I take a step back in shock.

His eyes soften. "Please. Hear me out."

"You have one minute," I say as I clench my jaw. I can't believe I'm giving him the light of day but– but, I need his help. I have no choice. And was this about his sister?

"Let me help you guys. I'll leave right after we kill the Sorcerer. I promise." Sincerity shines in his voice. "For the first time in a long time, I care about something, and I just can't walk away." I wonder if he was talking about killing the Sorcerer or something else. I saw how he looked at Wren.

"Can I please talk to her?" Quinn says softly.

The constant sorrow that I've been feeling since I lost Wren amplifies now, and it must show on my face because Quinn frowns.

"What's wrong?" he asks hesitantly, like he doesn't want to know the answer.

"She's not here," I mumble.

"What? What do you mean 'she's not here'?" Confusion shows on his face.

"He- he took her."

"What?" he asks again and then realization floods in. "No," he whispers. His face goes white and he trembles. "How?"

I tell him what happened that night, and he slowly sits down on a log. He puts his elbows on his knees and his face in his hands. A grim silence fills the space around us.

"It's my fault," he finally whispers through his hands.

I gulp. "Don't give yourself so much credit," I half-heartedly joke. "It was my fault as well. But I'm going to find her now."

Quinn looks up at me, and his face is set in determination. "I'm coming with you."

"I can't stop you." I have a feeling that he's going to tag along if I like it or not.

He gets up, and I start walking. "We should get going," I say over my shoulder.

"Wait, there's something else I need to tell you."

I turn back and look at him with suspicion. "What is it?"

"I brought someone who can help us get to the tower."

I jerk back and scan the trees. "You brought someone with you? Are you out of your mind?" I say vehemently.

"She's not here right now. I managed to lose her for a couple of seconds when I saw you, but it won't take long for her to find me."

I look at him, wondering if he's daft. "Who is she? Why did you bring her along? How can we trust her?"

"She knows her way around the forest, and she knows she can get there." He looks down at the ground before gazing back at me and adding, "We used to be close, though to answer your second question, we can't trust her. But we don't have another choice."

"You're making me second-guess my decision to let you help me, Quinn."

"We need her. She knows a faster way to the tower, and if what you tell me is true, then we have to get to Wren as soon as possible."

I open my mouth to speak when I hear the sound of footsteps and then a voice call out, "Quinn?"

Quinn looks at me, begging with his eyes.

I roll my eyes and nod, reluctantly accepting that his plan is better than my... well, nonexistent plan.

We both turn toward the voice, and I see a girl with raven hair and blue eyes staring at me with questions in her eyes. She wears a long black coat that goes down past her calves, covering a red blouse tucked into black trousers, and based on the way she holds herself, I know that, even though it doesn't seem like it, she probably has weapons hidden out of sight. She jerks her head at me and turns to Quinn. "Who's he?"

Quinn glances at me and then looks to her. "A friend. He's coming with us."

She frowns. "You didn't tell me about this."

"Well, it was by chance that I ran into him. The odds of it were really slim, so I didn't think it was important to mention." He frowns back at her. "I don't see what the problem is; if anything, he's useful to us."

She glances at me, and for a second I think I see concern in her expression before it disappears into a blank mask.

"Do you plan on telling me your name?" I ask after nobody speaks.

She stares blankly at me and Quinn sighs in frustration. "This is Tristan. Tristan, this is Zayne."

She shoots him a look of hatred before walking away. "Let's go."

I start walking with Quinn. "What is her problem?"

He looks at the ground, clearly uncomfortable. "We've had bad blood in the past, and I'm afraid it was my fault."

"I don't doubt that."

Quinn looks up. "I really am sorry. I- I've tried so hard to become a better person, but I seem to hurt whoever I grow close to."

He lets out a shaky laugh, absent of all humor, and for the first time, I see a glimpse of the sorrow and loneliness he hides from the rest of the world.

CHAPTER 46

QUINN

EVERY STEP SEEMS like torment as I think about what Zayne has told me. Wren is gone. I shudder with all that implicates. Who knows what's happening to her right now? If I had been here, maybe it would have been different, no matter what Zayne says to convince me otherwise. I try to imagine what I could have done differently, but nothing comes to mind. Maybe it just goes to prove that whatever I do injures good people. When I found Zayne in the forest, I was surprised he didn't kill me on sight.

I look at Zayne. "How was she? After I left?"

Zayne pauses and glances at me before returning his gaze to the path in front of us. "Not too good. You betrayed her trust." I flinch and Zayne sighs before offering me a tiny smile. "But she'll live."

A few quite moments pass before Zayne speaks again.

"So, what is the plan, anyway?" Zayne inquires. "The shortest way is across the river."

"Tristan told me that there was an even quicker way to the tower."

"She didn't tell you what it is."

"No, she didn't."

"That is concerning," Zayne says, frowning. "I'm still not comfortable with the idea of being dependent on her." He lets out a dry laugh. "What makes it worse is that I trust you more than I trust her." I push back a tree branch to keep walking, and he continues. "Why didn't you kill her?"

I glance up to make sure Tristan is a safe distance ahead of us before I answer, knowing that this question is inevitable. "What I told you was true. The Sorcerer pillaged my home with these black beasts. It was because my village was said to be a shelter for creatures of magic, but I've never seen them, since they stayed out of our way for the most part.

"My parents would always tell me stories of how our town was a safe haven, and it was our job to keep people safe because someone was after them. My father was the head of the village, but he insisted on living just like everyone else. Because he was an official, we had all the records and maps in our home, and that's why I knew the way to this forest.

"Anyway, the man who saved me was called Damien, and at the time, I hadn't realized the terrible things I was in for. It all started innocently enough, and he told my sister and I that he would take care of us, and that he would take us to his home. We listened to him because we didn't have a home anymore, and he had just saved our lives. But once we got there, I realized he was in charge of an assassin compound. And he wanted my sister and I to be a part of it.

"We resisted for a while, but then he started threatening us. So, we began training and learning our way around weapons. Over the years, I flourished because it was a way of forgetting that night, but my sister... my sister, she resisted. Damien was about to kill her, but I told him he would have to kill me too. I knew he wouldn't kill his best assassin, and I was right, but," I contort my face in pain. "He locked her up somewhere and says he'll kill her if I don't do as he says, or if I run away."

"So, I continued working for him and following his instructions. He sent me to find Wren because he wants her power, but then I met you guys. And for the first time in my life, I realized I could help in something good, something bigger. As we grew closer, you guys became my friends, and I hope you'll believe me when I say I would never think of killing Wren or you."

Zayne opens his mouth to say something else, but Tristan's voice calls out. "Come see this!"

We exchange a glance before hurrying to her side. The forest ends and reveals an empty clearing.

"What exactly are we supposed to be looking at?" Zayne asks her, confused.

"You'll see. Just be quiet," she says, while slowly making her way to the center of the clearing.

I take out my dagger, unsure of what she's up to.

She kneels down at the center of the clearing, reaches into her satchel, and takes out a giant stalk of some kind of plant. I tilt my head in confusion as she breaks the plant into pieces and arranges them in a pile at the center. Then she carefully backs up and joins us.

"Wha-" I start, but she cuts me off by putting a finger to her mouth. I grit my teeth and watch the clearing. Time passes and I'm about to demand to know what's happening, when a large shadow encompasses the area. I look up and a dark figure slowly descends into the clearing. Shock and panic clutch my heart. "What are you doing?" I ask her, bewildered.

The creature lands on the ground in a flourish of gold and starts to devour the plant she had laid out. As it's occupied, I take in the creature. It resembled a giant bird with a long tail trailing behind. Its golden feathers gleam as its wings rise in the sunlight, and its beak looks sharp. Tristan slowly walks up to the beast, and it immediately stills and regards her. As she gets closer, it tenses and lets out a squawk. She takes a cloth from her bag and quickly throws it onto the creature before it can react. Immediately, the beast calms down and lowers its head. Tristan looks back and gestures for us to come nearer.

"What is happening?" Zayne mutters, but we both start walking toward her.

"What is it?" I ask in awe.

"This is our ride," she says proudly, resting her hand on the animal.

Zayne starts coughing, and I look at her incredulously. "You're not serious, are you?"

She squints at us. "This is the fastest way to get to the tower. Any other way will take weeks, even months."

Zayne looks at it. "How will it take us to the tower? We can't just tell it where to go, if it even listens."

"The blanket is magic. Trust me, it will take us to the tower, so stop wasting time and get on."

I slowly approach as the animal glances at me, and I halt. Seeing that it's not going to attack, I slowly get on, with Zayne and Tristan soon to follow. I put a hand on the creature's neck, which rises and falls as it breathes, and then before I can react, the creature shoots up into the air. A scream sticks to my throat as we fly above the ground.

CHAPTER 47

WREN

I OPEN MY EYES in confusion and am met with a grey ceiling. I blink, perplexed, and sit up to look around. *Where am I?* I'm behind bars, in some sort of cell. Suddenly a memory flashes through me, that of a Ravager lunging at me before biting my arm. The reminder pulls my attention to the wound and, now that I'm aware of it, a searing pain travels through my body. I blanch at the sight of the wound and quickly turn my head away, trying to ignore it.

I have seen a Ravager. Downright fear threatens to pull me under, or else I would have been amazed. As I think about the incident, I remember the familiar symbol I had spied on its shoulder. I jolt and quickly stand up. It was the sign of the Sorcerer. I am in the tower.

I frantically try to call upon my power, but I feel a mental block, like when I have used too much magic at once. Looking down, I see a black band around my forearm, with the Sorcerer's symbol engraved into it. I tug at it, but it doesn't budge. Giving up, I try to push back the fear and think about my situation. The goal was to come here in the first place, wasn't it? But now I don't have the element of surprise, and I am locked in a cell as a prisoner. To add onto that, I don't have Zayne with me. What am I going to do? I'm alone.

Without warning, a sound echoes off the stone, and my breath catches. I strain to pinpoint the sound, and hear the steady thump of someone walking toward me in the hallway outside my cell. The sound begins to get louder, and I back into the wall as my chest starts moving up and down in panic. Staring at the darkened hallway beyond the bars of the cell, I wait for my fate.

A shadow appears on the other side of the bars, and my heart stops as it gradually steps into the light. A cloaked figure moves toward me and opens its hand to reveal a key. Taking the key, it slowly unlocks the prison door, which swings open with a creak. No sparing a word, the creature approaches me with a hand reached out.

I jolt out of its reach, but I'm not fast enough as it grabs onto my shirt and pulls me forward. I twist and thrash, trying to break free, but nothing works. I reach in for my magic once again but find emptiness. The figure grips my forearm tightly and yanks me down the hallway. I look into the other prison cells, but they are all empty.

We climb a narrow set of stairs, and before I know it, we enter a large room. I look around for any exits, but see none. The figure proceeds to another narrow set of staircases against the wall, dragging me with him. As we walk up, the steps turn to the right every time, and I realize that the staircases wraps around the tower. Just as I imagine that the climb is never going to end, we go around another curve to reveal a black door.

The door opens without a clank and I feel something push me from behind. I tumble to the floor with a grimace and look up to the see the door closing behind me. Carefully, I get up and look around. Black marble covers the entire room and giant pillars are set against the walls. I feel a cold breeze against my face, and when I turn, I spy a wide space in the wall, revealing the large balcony we had seen on the cliff. The only sound in the room is the swish of the curtains as they move with the wind. Choking on my panic, I realize that it's the same place of my nightmare.

Hands shaking, my attention is drawn to the black throne at the back of the room. It appears to be made of the same marble as the rest of the enclosure, but also has threads of gold weaved into it. As I focus on the throne, I realize there is something seated on it. My eyes adjust to the dark, and I realize with a start that it's a person.

That's the moment I know it is him. The Sorcerer.

It's as though time itself has stopped as the Sorcerer approaches. I feel sudden fear and almost cast my eyes down, but I cannot seem weak. I set my shoulders back and finally look at the person in the face. Cold eyes of onyx stare at me, and I feel sudden dark power threatening to crush down upon me. I let out a shaky breath and force myself to scan the person's entire face. A man in his mid-fifties stares back at me. Oddly enough, even though he looks aged, no wrinkles carve into his face. Instead, he appears to be a picture come to life. I frown, as faint recognition flits through my mind. I've seen him before, but where?

"Hello, Wren," the man says. His voice is deep and holds a subtle edge of danger.

I raise my chin defiantly. "How do you know my name?"

"Oh, Wren." He laughs. "I know everything about you, even things you yourself don't know."

I say nothing and he tilts his head in question.

"Do you not know who I am?"

I squint. "You…" Sudden recognition hits me. "It's not possible," I choke out. "How are you still alive?"

"Everything will come to light, soon. But wouldn't you want your friends to be here as well?"

My eyebrows draw together. "What?"

He leans his head toward the balcony and, as I turn, an object falls onto its marble floor in a blur of gold. I blink and, with numb shock, realize that it is a creature. It reminds me of a bird as its gold feathers shimmer in the daylight, in stark contrast to the darkness inside the tower. I almost forget about the Sorcerer when three figures dismount.

Relief flashes through me as I recognize Zayne. I lunge toward him, but the man grabs my shoulder. I struggle, but his grip is like iron. Zayne looks up and meets my eyes. Immense relief shows in his face.

"Wren?" He rushes toward me, but abruptly stops when he spies the man next to me. Anger flashes through his expression as he pulls free his sword. Quickly, I see recognition flit across his face.

"I can't believe it," he whispers.

"Zayne!" A familiar voice calls out and my heart stops beating. I glance behind Zayne to see Quinn running up to us. He comes to a halt and his eyes widen as he takes me in. "Wren?" Though I know I shouldn't, I feel relief at seeing him here.

"H- how did you guys get here?" I ask, confused.

Quinn gives a gentle smile. "I got help from a friend."

"Hmm, I wouldn't consider us friends." A girl steps up next to him, and there's something in her eyes that instantly makes me wary.

"Good work, Tristan. You may go," says the man next to me, and Tristan nods before mounting the creature and taking off once again.

I glance at Quinn, and his face contorts into a picture of anger.

Yet, before anyone can react to what has just happened, the man speaks again. "Ah, the tiny trio. Reunited once again." He lets go of my shoulder and I hurry toward Zayne, who welcomes me with relief and touches my arm.

"Are you okay?"

I nod quickly, ignoring Quinn's imploring gaze.

Quinn faces the Sorcerer, looking at him closely for the first time. "I know you from somewhere." He frowns, "But where?" His eyes suddenly widen. "You're King Alberich."

King Alberich gives a sickly smile. "Glad to know people still know who I am."

I grimace in disgust. Who wouldn't? His face is plastered over hundreds of books. My fear slightly lessens with Zayne and Quinn's presence. I step forward. "How are you still alive?"

"The essence of humans can keep you alive for a very long time," Alberich sneers.

Bile climbs up my throat as I think about what he's implying.

Zayne lets out an disbelieving scoff. "That's what they were killed for? The people that you murdered?"

The king tilts his head. "Of course not. I also collected their shadows."

His words slowly register with me and, red flashes in my eyes, I slowly understand what he's saying. I had always doubted it, not knowing if it could be true. Confirming it returned a fresh wave of pain. "You're in control of the shadows that killed my aunt," I say in rage.

He frowns as he shifts his gaze to me. "Ah, yes. Your necklace stopped them from getting too close. The Lochaere in its entirety is more powerful than I had imagined."

I hold back tears and glare at the king. "You won't get away with this."

King Alberich lets out a cold laugh. "Silly Wren, you've followed my plan all along. You're here, aren't you?"

I flinch. "Why would you want me here?"

"It wasn't only you I wanted here. I also wanted him." He points and I follow his hand.

CHAPTER 48

ZAYNE

ONCE I REGISTER that he is pointing at me, I take a cautionary step back. "What are you talking about?"

"Oh, you have no idea." King Alberich looks between us with mock disbelief. "Well, it's no surprise to Wren or you that you have magic." I glance sharply at Wren. She knows? "But what you don't know is so much bigger than that. Zayne's magic has more potential and-" He grins. "-raw power than I have ever seen before. *The* Enchanter's Child." He addresses Wren, "Why, I wonder, did that magnitude not pass to you as well, Wren? He is your brother after all."

My ears buzz and I feel the room tilt before I fall onto my knees. It can't be. "You're lying."

Alberich tuts, "I would have no motive. Besides, I think you know it in your heart. The power that you hold as well as your relation to Wren. I bet when you first saw her, you felt a hint of recognition, did you not?"

"But he has a family," Wren whispers.

"Your parents saw the power in him and thought it was best to hand him over to someone they could trust, the royal family of Elrea. Your parents worked with them to keep their kingdom safe." I stare at the black floor in disbelief as I think about the many times I had joked with my brother, saying I didn't look like anyone in my family.

"Then shouldn't you fear for your life?" Quinn asks when nobody speaks. "You have just admitted that he is more powerful than you are."

"Ah, and the infamous Black Assassin," Alberich says, swiveling his attention to Quinn. "I have heard much about you."

CHAPTER 49

QUINN

I STARE AT HIM coolly. "You killed my parents."

He gives out a loud laugh before giving a short tsk.

Returning my gaze and starts to murmur words under his breath. Suddenly, a flash of memories zip through my mind, but I immediately know they aren't mine.

The first one is in this very room and I am kneeling before the throne. King Alberich is seated in the place of honor, looking down at me. "A deal is a deal. Some of your assassins, to find people so I can steal their essences, in exchange for my beasts."

The castle fades and is replaced by villages. Damien is there. He kneels down and talks to the beasts. "Spare the children."

Then the memories span and show Damien taking away various children, explaining to their tear-stained faces that he was there to save them, sending them to his Compound.

As quickly as they arrived, the memories fade away, and I am back in the present. I stumble back in shock. It was Damien all along.

Alberich frowns. "And he attempted to stab me in the back by asking you to find the Enchanters' Child. Someone you had mistaken Wren to be. You didn't even consider Zayne, did you?" He shakes his head. "I must admit, I'm a little disappointed. I have heard great things about you."

CHAPTER 50

WREN

I STARE IN SHOCK at King Alberich as he talks to Quinn. Why would he want us here? Understanding hits me. He wouldn't be so concerned with Zayne if the prince wasn't a threat.

I flashback to the first time I had seen the Sorcerer, or his shadow, as he stole the essence from my parents. He's planning to steal our essences, I realize with dread. Then there will be no one to stop him; we are the last of the Arobol.

I see King Alberich focus on something behind me with intensity, and I turn in panic to see Zayne transfixed in a state of shock, gazing at the floor. I look down to the black band on my forearm and start tugging at it to no avail. I shout a warning at Zayne and he looks up slowly, seeming to break out of his trance, but it's too late. King Alberich reaches out his hand and starts muttering. Gradually, bright red emits from the king's chest and Zayne tilts his head back with pain. His face is set in a grimace and I suddenly think of the line from my mother's book. *He had to make a sacrifice. The Ravager vanished like shadows retreating when there is light.*

I clutch at the Lochaere around my neck, and it glows blue with my touch. The black band is inhibiting my magic, but it doesn't mean that my magic isn't there. I grit my teeth with resolve, hoping this works. I slowly begin to walk toward the Sorcerer and the Lochaere glows even brighter. I reach inside myself and fight against the block, trying to reach for my magic.

My magic doesn't belong to anyone but me; there has to be a way to reach it. I delve in, and my breath catches when I sense the familiar ball of energy. I grasp at it and, at first, it's like clutching at water. But finally, I'm able to grab it.

I grin in relief as the block disappears. The black band severs and falls to the ground as I continue walking. Focused on Zayne, Alberich doesn't notice how close I am until it's too late. I reach into myself and find as much magic as I can, and then it's as though I'm doused in flames. A blue light emits around me and King Alberich stares with horror as I reach toward the red emitting from his chest, knowing I can't survive this.

As soon as I touch his chest, a pain, greater than I ever thought possible, sears through me. I feel something inside me break, but I keep my hold steady. Alberich stares at his chest in horror. He looks at me.

"What have you done?" he screams as cracks appear in his body like he's made of china. I push forward with everything I have, and King Alberich shatters into pieces of glass that fall to the marble floor.

I grin in relief, knowing that even if I'm going to die, I have achieved what I came to achieve. The last things I remember before the darkness are Zayne and Quinn, shouting.

CHAPTER 51

ZAYNE

I DASH TO WREN in horror, trying to wrap my mind around what has just happened. She saved my life. Quinn reaches her before me and gently puts Wren's head in his lap.

"Come on, wake up!" he says, but Wren remains still.

I grab her wrist and check her pulse. I hold my breath, hoping for a miracle, and I feel a feather-light thrumming. With faith, I keep my hand on her wrist, hoping I hadn't imagined it, and laugh with tears in my eyes when I realize that her heart's still beating. I look at Quinn.

"She's still alive," I say, and his shoulders sag with relief as he holds her tighter. "But she's dying," I say sadly.

Quinn looks at me. "There has to be something we can do."

I furrow my eyebrows as I glance down at her. "I- I have an idea, but it might not work."

"Do it," Quinn says with resolve.

I gently lay my hand on her chest and try to reach inside to find the... magic that I know is there. But when I try, there is nothing. I look at Wren's face, my sister's, and try again. I try to find the energy I had felt when I started the fire at the gypsy camp. I probe in my mind, thinking that maybe there's nothing there, but just when I'm about to give up, I feel a small ball of energy.

Carefully, I reach for it, trying to be delicate, knowing that a misstep will cause me to use all of it, and not in a small dose. When I touch the energy, I feel a sudden warmth in my chest and gradually try to direct the energy to my hand. Slowly but steadily, my palm starts to warm and emits a light blue glow. I watch in amazement, but still nothing happens. I take a nervous breath before putting a little more energy into Wren. Her body jerks, and I take my hand off in panic. Quinn looks at me in alarm before he checks her wrist again. He gasps in disbelief.

"Her pulse is stronger. Do it again." I repeat what I had done, and suddenly Wren jerks up with a gasp.

My breath stops as I grasp her hand in elation.

Quinn wipes away a tear and clasps her shoulder. "We thought you were dead."

Wren gives a laugh of disbelief as tears run down my face. "That's because I'm supposed to be." She frowns. "But my magic- I can't feel it anymore."

I try to think about the implications of that, but I squeeze her hand. "We'll think about it later. The important thing is you're alive."

She shakes her head in disbelief. "It's really over. He's gone." She hugs us with shaking arms. "It's over."

As the words leave her mouth, a small hum fills the air. At first, it's easy to ignore, but it slowly gets louder. We all cover our ears and stand as we look around the room. Just as the hum seems to get unbearably loud, a boom resonates through the throne room, and the first sound immediately ceases. My eye catches on something golden at the center of the room. I see that it is a book. I walk toward it cautiously.

The cover of the book is gold, and emblazoned on it in silver are the words, 'The Enchanters' Child'. I hear footsteps as Wren and Quinn follow me to see what I'm inspecting.

"What is it?" Quinn asks.

I frown. "I have no clue."

I slowly open the front cover and see that the first page read, 'Chapter 1, Wren.'

I hear a small gasp from Wren on my right and I slowly flip through the pages in awe. The story is filled with what has happened to each of us and our stories.

"This must be how 'The Forgotten Gift' came to existence as well."

Quinn lets out a grunt of disbelief. "That means our stories are in here?"

"How does the book end, Zayne?" Wren asks.

Holding my breath, I flip to the last page, and the final line leaves my blood cold.

After finally defeating the Sorcerer, the three believed they were safe, but little did they know, there was an even darker magic slowly growing.

ABOUT THE AUTHOR

Navya Sarikonda is a young author from Atlanta. The Enchanters' Child is her first novel which was started when she was twelve. In addition to this novel, Navya has written several short stories. When she is not writing, she can be found reading or playing the piano and flute.

www.NavyaSarikonda.com

CPSIA information can be obtained
at www.ICGtesting.com
Printed in the USA
BVHW032344080719
552916BV00006B/29/P